CUSTOMER
SERVICE
EXCELLENCE

CSE

Kent
County
Council
kent.gov.uk

SPECIAL MESSAGE TO READERS

THE ULVERSCROFT FOUNDATION (registered UK charity number 264873)

was established in 1972 to provide funds for research, diagnosis and treatment of eye diseases. Examples of major projects funded by the Ulverscroft Foundation are:-

- The Children's Eye Unit at Moorfields Eye Hospital, London
- The Ulverscroft Children's Eye Unit at Great Ormond Street Hospital for Sick Children
- Funding research into eye diseases and treatment at the Department of Ophthalmology, University of Leicester
- The Ulverscroft Vision Research Group, Institute of Child Health
- Twin operating theatres at the Western Ophthalmic Hospital, London
- The Chair of Ophthalmology at the Royal Australian College of Ophthalmologists

You can help further the work of the Foundation by making a donation or leaving a legacy. Every contribution is gratefully received. If you would like to help support the Foundation or require further information, please contact:

THE ULVERSCROFT FOUNDATION
The Green, Bradgate Road, Anstey
Leicester LE7 7FU, England
Tel: (0116) 236 4325

website: www.foundation.ulverscroft.com

THE ENVIED AND OTHER STORIES

A dead scientist's undamaged brain is transplanted into a robot body and kept alive. Soon, other people who die in their turn come to inhabit the continually improving grey cases. But why do they sever all contact with their former friends and family members? Warren and his girlfriend Judith are both envious and suspicious of the way in which the Greys are taking control of society, and determined to discover their secrets. Then Judith dies and becomes a Grey . . . Five stories of the fantastic and the supernatural by John Burke.

Books by John Burke
in the Linford Mystery Library:

THE GOLDEN HORNS
THE POISON CUPBOARD
THE DARK GATEWAY
FEAR BY INSTALMENTS
MURDER, MYSTERY AND MAGIC
ONLY THE RUTHLESS CAN PLAY
THE KILL DOG
THE NIGHTMARE WHISPERERS
ECHO OF BARBARA
THE DEVIL'S FOOTSTEPS
TEACH YOURSELF TREACHERY
THE TWISTED TONGUES
THE BLACK CHARADE
LADYGROVE
DEAD LETTERS
DREAMS, DEMONS AND DEATH

JOHN BURKE

THE ENVIED
AND OTHER STORIES

Complete and Unabridged

LINFORD
Leicester

First published in Great Britain in 1954

First Linford Edition
published 2015

*A catalogue record for this book is available
from the British Library.*

ISBN 978–1–4448–2338–7

Published by
F. A. Thorpe (Publishing)
Anstey, Leicestershire

Set by Words & Graphics Ltd.
Anstey, Leicestershire
Printed and bound in Great Britain by
T. J. International Ltd., Padstow, Cornwall

This book is printed on acid-free paper

Contents

THE ENVIED

The small group of grey figures had marched solemnly across the paveway in front of them, and had been snatched away in a fast helicar. Now they were left with that familiar feeling of resentment. The arrogance of those grey creatures — their remoteness — their indescribable aura of autocratic indifference . . .

Warren said: 'If we could only find some way of getting at them! If only there was just one of them on our side.'

'But there isn't,' said Judith.

'Or if there is, the rest of them take darned good care that there shan't be any contact.'

'I don't believe there's even one of them who'd help us,' said Judith gravely. 'Once you become a Grey, you lose all interest in your old friends.' Her voice was always grave in that thoughtful, gently melancholy way. Warren glanced down at her as she turned her smooth, solemn little face towards him; and, not for the first time, he thanked his lucky stars that he'd got a girl with some intelligence instead of one of those bright giggling creatures who were always in pursuit of a good time. A good time . . . when the human race was being gradually throttled by the domineering Greys! It didn't bear thinking of.

The two of them stepped off the moving paveway at a junction, and waited for the intersection belt to start up again. While they waited, two Greys came out of the massive building on the other side of the carriageway and stood for a moment at the top of the steps. Warren put his hand lightly on Judith's arm and directed her attention towards those impassive figures.

'That's one of their exclusive clubs,' he said in a low voice. 'What do they get up to in there? Why are they so afraid of letting the rest of us find out?'

These were not new questions. They were old ones: but they never grew stale. The sight of the blank, withdrawn features of a Grey could always provoke that angry enquiry once more. Now, as so many times before, two ordinary human beings stared at the non-committal features of their rulers, and wondered — wondered irritably, bitterly, suspiciously.

Judith said: 'If you became a Grey — if you died today and they took you over — would you forget me?'

'You know I wouldn't.'

'But other people have forgotten. They've been taken over, and never returned even to pass the time of day with their families or friends.'

The paveway clicked as relays tripped, and the cross-town belt began to move swiftly. Warren steered Judith into the middle of the crowd of people coming along. 'I wonder if they have all forgotten, really?' he said as they went on. 'I mean, how do we know there haven't been lots of men and women who've objected to being made into soulless machines? Maybe the awkward ones are sent off to the planets, where there aren't any normal human beings to be friends with, anyway. We don't know.'

'So many things we don't know,' sighed

Judith, 'and no way of finding out.'

They fell into a despondent silence. Warren turned over in his mind a multitude of plans for breaking the spell of the Greys. They had been flesh and blood themselves once, hadn't they? They had no right to become so lofty and to reserve so many privileges for themselves simply because they had died. If only there were some way of being turned into a Grey without losing one's sense of loyalty to the ordinary, decent people of the world.

Warren said abruptly: 'Sometimes think I ought to — well, throw myself under a monocar, so that I could get into the middle of the Greys.'

Judith went pale. 'Don't talk like that!'

'But what other way is there of getting at them?'

'If you did that,' she said, 'you'd become just like the rest of them.'

'I wouldn't.'

'How can you be sure? If they offered you privileges and . . . and . . . well, whatever it is they've got that makes them so high-and-mighty . . . '

'There must be some way of resisting that sort of thing. If you really set your mind to it.'

She shook her head. She was just as idealistic as he was, but she was practical with it: she had seen her father killed in an accident, seen him taken away, and been to the Conversion Ward two days later. He had repudiated her. Not contemptuously or unpleasantly: he had just made it clear that he was somehow different, and that there was no contact between them anymore. For a while she had seemed to detect some struggle going on in him. For a while she had continued to see him, but he had gone further and further away from her, his whole spirit and personality receding behind that grey robot mask.

Then there had been her mother. And one or two friends had gone from her. She had no illusions now. When you became a Grey, you cut yourself off from what you had once been.

The paveway slowed, and they stepped off onto the fixed lane. Saturn Square lay spread out before them, with its great blocks of administrative offices and the mighty edifice of the World Theatre. The centre of the universe, they called this. They said that if you stood here long enough, everybody in the universe would sooner or later walk or ride past you. But that was one of those sayings, and nothing more. Even if it were true, would you be able to tell the difference between one being and another? All the creatures that came back from Mars and Venus, or the bleak moons of the farther worlds, were Greys: and one Grey looked just like another. There were no personal relationships. There was nothing that was warm and human — or, if there was, it wasn't shared with the lower classes, the poor downtrodden unfortunates who were still alive in their original flesh and blood form.

'That building there makes me dizzy,' said Judith, craning her neck and staring up. 'It makes me want to fall backwards — '

'Be careful! Judith!'

Warren gave a sudden shout and tried to grab her. But she had stepped a pace back, staggering, and was out over the edge of the paveway as a fast monocar sped round the edge of the square.

It was on her in a second, and over her. There was the puff of its brakes, and a babble of agitated conversation. A crowd gathered.

Warren knelt beside her, saying: 'No, Judith, no,' and touching her face. Blood seeped out from under her summer dress. Everyone else was jostling and talking. But Judith lay still, her face blank, strangely peaceful . . . and quite, quite empty of all that had been there only a few moment ago.

The hospital car dropped from the sky, twisting down between the great towers of the square like a falling leaf. Two impassive Greys got out and lifted Judith.

Warren said: 'I want to come with you.'

One of them turned its neatly etched, expressionless face towards him. The rectangular mouth moved. The steady voice, with hardly any inflection, said: 'It is not advisable.'

'I tell you I want to come. You must try to save her — '

'Save her?' said the metallic echo. 'Perhaps we do not mean the same thing by the words. But you need not worry. She will be dealt with very well.'

'Isn't there any chance?'

'Chance?' The echo sounded almost mocking. 'She has every chance. Her brain is probably undamaged. We shall take her over.'

'But . . . ' It was no use. What could he possibly say?

The crowd murmured. Their buzz of restrained sound was like a resonance set off by his own despondency.

Now Judith was stowed away inside the hospital car. She was gone. Warren leaned forward as though to rush the car, to put up a fight and take her back.

The Grey who had spoken to him before said: 'You were a friend of hers?'

'Yes. She and I . . . I mean . . . '

'Never mind. It is of no consequence. All we require is her name and address for record purposes. We will check on all other necessary details.'

Warren made an abrupt decision. He said: 'I'll tell you the name and address when we get to the hospital.'

'It is better if you do not come.'

'If I ask to come, you can't stop me, can you?'

There was no anger, no emotion whatever, in the measured reply. 'We could stop you if we wished. But it is not normal. If you insist, we will take you. But for your own sake it is better to go away and forget.'

'I'm coming,' said Warren.

'Very well. In front, beside the driver, please.'

Warren felt cold as he got in beside the motionless figure of the driver. There was nothing real and human about these creatures. Perhaps he was a fool to put himself in their power. Then he smiled wryly. After all, wasn't the human race entirely in their power: wasn't this whole system something that human beings had themselves created and brought upon themselves?

The car rose with breathtaking swiftness, and the towers and spires of the city reeled away beneath.

Warren had acted purely on impulse,

but now a thousand confused plans began to froth wildly inside his head. The Judith he had known was dead; but there would soon be another Judith, and might he not be able to get in touch with her? Perhaps *if* he insisted on remaining with her, or at any rate visiting her frequently in those early stages, he would be able to prevent her from drifting away as so many human beings drifted when they had been transmuted. Whatever it was that the Greys did to cancel out old loyalties, he must be there to combat it. His mind had always been in tune with Judith's. Perhaps there would still be a link — enough to give him a hold, however precarious, on her.

The driver began to talk to him unexpectedly. His sentences were brief and impersonal, as though he were reciting a carefully memorised lesson. 'You don't want to pursue this too far. Be wise. Your friend will forget when she begins her new life. You will forget, unless you are foolish enough to make yourself go on remembering.'

'I don't see,' said Warren challengingly,

‘why people who have known one another for a long time shouldn’t keep in touch.’

‘That is because you not understand.’

‘Does anybody? A normal person, that is? If you don’t make it your business to explain to us — ’

‘Many things have been explained,’ came the bland reply.

‘Oh yes, lots of things. Official handouts: we’ve had plenty of those. No ordinary human being can fly to planets because his body won’t stand up to the strain. His metabolism would let him down on other worlds. And that’s why the Greys do all the hard work on their own. The Greys have a more detached viewpoint than the rest of us, so they’ve taken law-making and government into their own hands.’

‘We are aware of these facts,’ said the voice, with no trace of irony. ‘They are facts. You should accept them, because they are true.’

Warren snorted, then remained silent as the car fell swiftly to rest before the roof entrance of the hospital. Efficient, soundless Greys took Judith inside in a matter of seconds. He followed. There was a lift, then a corridor along which he moved in company with three Greys who did not speak to him, and then a room in which he waited for a long time, watching unseeingly the news flashes on the wall visor.

At last the door slid open. A tall Grey with long, bare, incredibly flexible fingers came in. Warren got up.

The Grey said: 'Your friend is well.'

For a moment a wild hope surged up in Warren's mind. 'She's well? You mean she's going to be all right? I mean — '

'I mean that the operation has been successful. The transfer has been accomplished.'

Warren slumped back into his chair. 'I see,' he said bleakly. 'She's . . . one of you now.'

'Yes. She is one of us now.'

* * *

The gift of what amounted almost to immortality seemed at first one of the greatest benefits that had ever been bestowed on mankind. There had, of course, been no promise by scientists of immortality. A thousand years in most cases, with perhaps some extensions to two thousand years: that was the extent of their original estimate. But a thousand years was immortality to a being who had regarded a hundred as the ultimate probable limit. It did not matter that the ordinary body had to be discarded: the wretched inadequate body with its aches and pains and imperfections.

The first robot carriers had been clumsy, but the brains which had been mounted in them soon took possession and adapted the robot facilities. Within a few years a greater flexibility had been achieved. A great scientist died. His brain was carefully removed, revived by the action of focussed cosmic rays in conjunction with the original Murchison apparatus, and inserted in the open head of the robot that had been designed for its reception. In a matter of months the scientist was at work again, with new powers. The mechanical body never grew tired; the fingers were more flexible and less prone to damage than those fingers which had so recently been cremated; the mind was sharper and more deliberate. The scientist's mind grappled with the problems of its new body, made suggestions for modifications, and offered more and more scope to those people who came after — those people who died in their turn and, in their turn, came to inhabit the continually improving cases which were being manufactured for them.

With the prospect of so many years ahead, doctors and philosophers felt that they could expand. Time was unlimited. Their own thought processes were somehow quickened now that they were freed from the encumbrance of bone, flesh and blood, and research developed rapidly. Not only were the robot carriers perfected, but cures for human ailments were devised by the newly liberated brains. The span of human life was extended; and when at last the end came, the brain was removed and, after two brief hours in the Murchison regeneration apparatus, settled into its new home. The life of the mind went on.

At first people were rather shy of admitting to the existence of the robots. Originally they were dubbed 'the Aftermen,' but this clumsy phrase could not stick for long; in due course the grey plastic covering of the artificial bodies resulted in their being called Greys. There was at that time no emotional undertone to the word. It was only as generations went by that the Greys became associated with tyranny and greed and exclusiveness.

Only the Greys could withstand the prolonged flights associated with travel to the planets. The radiation from solar flares, plus the unleashed, unshielded power of cosmic rays out in space made interplanetary travel impossible for normal human beings. The living conditions on the other planets were, in any case, quite unbearable. What a blessing, it was said at first, was the introduction of the new race.

But resentment grew. The Greys were too clever. Not only did they travel through interplanetary space, bringing back valuable minerals on whose disposal they made their own decisions: they began to displace ordinary human beings on the councils of the world, claiming that this was for the benefit of everyone. They were more intelligent and more dispassionate than their flesh and blood predecessors. But, they gently argued, they understood human problems: had they not, themselves, once been ordinary creatures? The minds that now made decrees, that carried on abstruse researches and dealt with the new problems of the planets, were human minds that simply went on living and growing in wisdom.

'The development of the After-men,' said one of the early Greys in a speech made to the Council of the World Federation, 'is the development of the whole human race. What we do is for the mutual benefit of the primitives and for ourselves: indeed, it could be said that the primitives benefit more than we do, since our pleasure is mainly in study and abstract thought, yet we work gladly for the bodily comfort of those whose minds will one day join our community.'

It sounded very fine. It was the standard argument, the official viewpoint; but there were some who distrusted the use of certain words. There seemed to be a slur in that description — 'primitives.' The Greys were setting themselves up as aristocrats.

In the middle of the twenty-second century there was a revolution in Central Europe. The group that had once, as a nation, been known as Czechoslovakia, declared its opposition to the growing power of the Greys. It objected to certain decrees regarding the readjustment of Federation control boundaries and limitations that had been placed on ordinary human research into infra-atomics.

'*The Greys*', ran the proclamation, '*wish to hold all power in their inhuman hands. The peoples of the human race must unite and assert their independence.*'

There was certainly a hubbub in scientific circles. And there was a great deal of angry speculation when two leading human scientists died in suspicious circumstances and were taken into the After-men fold. From there they declared that they had been mistaken in advocating opposition to the Greys. The

Greys were enlightened rulers who thought only in terms of the welfare of the race from which, after all, they sprang.

Nevertheless there was an armed insurrection, culminating in an attempt to take over the big research laboratories in Prague. The Greys defeated this easily enough, with very little bloodshed. They ordered, however, judicial execution of the four ringleaders . . . and within a matter of days the converted minds of the ringleaders were uttering, through robot mouths, the recantation of their earlier beliefs.

The situation was a disturbed one, but there was no sign of an open conflict. The arguments of the Greys were very convincing. Even if you had doubts, you had to admit that on the face of things they were doing a good job.

Human life had been prolonged and made easier. The worst diseases had been conquered. Imports from the exploited planets made existence easier in many ways: food supplies and innumerable constructional materials came to swell the riches of Earth. Work was not onerous. There was more leisure than there had ever been. Leisure and independence.

Independence. In some meanings of the word, that was.

There was no ban on the expression of opinion, and the only restrictions the Greys imposed were on matters that did not greatly concern the general public: infra-atomics and the management of interplanetary freight must not be left in the hands of ordinary people. There was a sound explanation; for every law and regulation there was always a neat, reasonably coherent explanation. If you were satisfied with a fairly luxurious, pleasurable existence, you had no real need to ask awkward questions. Let the Greys look after administration if they wanted to. There was sport; there were the telestadia, the new dances, the sensual new music, and all the joys of an efficiently organised, enlightened civilisation.

Provided you didn't ask awkward questions.

Provided you didn't want to know

how and why people's minds changed when they had been removed from the mortal body and settled into the robot carriers.

* * *

Warren looked at the mathematical regularity of the Grey doctor's features and said: 'What happens to Judith now? What's it like for her?'

'It would be difficult to make you understand.'

'You could try.'

'We have tried many times before, without any great success. It is better to accept that a change has taken place. In time you yourself will qualify for admission to a carrier, and then you will know all that you wish to know.'

'Why shouldn't I know now?' Warren persisted, with a feeling that if he did not keep talking now something essential would slip through his fingers. 'Judith means a lot to me. If I can see her — '

'Not yet.'

'But you're not going to forbid me to

see her? If I come in tomorrow, I can talk to her?'

'She will not be interested,' said the Grey coldly.

'That remains to be seen. What do you do to people? Why do you try to drag them away from their friends — from people who love them?'

'You loved this woman?'

Unexpectedly, Warren found himself hesitating. Of course he loved Judith. Not in any silly, sentimental way: he and she had shared their views for years, and been very close to one another; they had planned to oppose the Greys one day, and go down in history as benefactors and liberators of the human race. Judith had greedily drunk in everything he had said to her. Of course he had loved her. Their minds had been in tune. There was no reason why they should not still be in tune.

He said: 'Yes. I loved her.'

'You will find someone else,' said the Grey.

Warren was furious. He could have struck the creature. But what was the use of striking a creature of metal and plastic? 'I don't want anyone else,' he said. 'I want to see Judith. As soon as I can.'

'Very well. You can come tomorrow afternoon, sixteen hours. But do not expect too much.'

Warren did not reply to this. He went past the Grey with only the curtest of farewells, and was soon outside in the fresh air. The outside world seemed to come up and hit him. Only now, away from that building, did he realise that Judith was actually dead. Dead. It was a word you didn't use often nowadays: you said so-and-so had been transferred, or taken over. But when you felt bitterly about the Greys, regarding them as enemies, the older word came back into use.

Judith was dead.

But he would talk to her again tomorrow.

* * *

The hours seemed endless. He lay awake for most of the night, listening to the subdued noises of the purring, smoothly running city. It was almost as though he could hear the gears engaging, the switches clicking. Everything was so well-organised. Life was neat; human beings were comfortably provided for. And at the top, running the whole thing for their own ends, were these inscrutable Greys, who ceased to be human once they had gone through the process of transference.

Their own ends . . . whatever those might be.

It was a question that Judith must answer. Lying awake, Warren tried to reduce his plans to some sort of order. He must not fumble or hesitate or make a false step right at the beginning.

The following afternoon he made his way to the hospital. It looked uninviting. It did not welcome healthy human beings, particularly when they came with challenges on their lips. He was silently ushered along a corridor, into a lift again, and then through a doorway into a quiet ward. There was, oddly, none of the antiseptic smell he had expected — the smell one usually associated with hospital wards. Here there was only a faint dry breath of something metallic. Like a machine-shop, he thought with a tingle of horror.

The beds were not really beds. They were inclined couches, padded with some springy material. There were no sheets and blankets, and no temperature stabilisation plugs. It was an austere room.

Warren approached the tilted couch that had been indicated to him. A grey face looked up at him from a grey, shapeless body. He licked his lips, trying not to show the sudden, unexpected revulsion he felt, and said: 'Hello, Judith.'

There was a long pause. Then the mouth moved as though still unsure of its own function. 'Hello, Warren.'

'You recognise me?' he said eagerly. 'You remember. You haven't forgotten me — and you're not going to, are you?'

The reply was measured and unemotional. 'I have not forgotten you. Not yet.'

'And you're not going to,' he repeated.

Superimposed on the standard Grey features he seemed to see, for a fleeting second, the features of Judith, and he was overcome by an appalling sense of loss. It was worse than it had been during his tormented, sleepless night. He felt somehow that he had failed, that he and Judith had never truly lived . . . and now she was gone, and he was talking to a ghost.

He tried to pull himself together. There was a job to be done; a campaign to be begun. He said: 'How do you feel? What's it like?'

'I cannot tell you. You would not understand.'

'Now look,' snapped Warren, 'don't you start that! You don't want to get into Grey habits right away do you? Can't you give me some idea — help me to get some glimmering of what goes on? Remember all the things we planned; all the things we said we'd do if we became Greys . . . ? We were going to put the ordinary human beings first, remember?'

A pause, then: 'Yes. I remember.'

'Well, then?'

'But now it is different.'

'You're like all the rest of them. They've promised you something big — dangled presents in front of you — offered you a good job, I suppose.'

'It is not like that.'

The indifference of the voice exasperated him. It was with the greatest difficulty that he curbed his temper and, in a carefully controlled tone, said: 'I thought up some plans last night. I lay awake all night, Judith. I had to do something to save myself from going mad. And all I could think of was that we mustn't get out of touch.'

There was no nod, no sound, no movement of sympathy.

'We must try to break the spell of the Greys,' he went on. 'You've got to resist anything they try to put over. If you keep in touch with me . . . '

For some reason he found himself speaking slowly and deliberately, as though trying to put something across to a rather stupid person who was incapable of sustained concentration. No. No, it wasn't like that at all. Rather, it was as though he were a child trying to attract the attention of someone older and wiser — someone who was really too busy to listen, who didn't want to be bothered. That spurred him on. Judith was already in danger of succumbing to the Grey influence. He had to bring back to her mind the intensity and sincerity of those old plans and discussions they had had.

'I'll come and see you every day,' he said. 'You must tell me everything that happens to you. I'll keep a detailed check on all you tell me. And then if they try to lure you away, I will at least have a lead on what's happening. I can follow up. I can get some notion of what it is the Greys are up to.'

'Others have tried,' was the response.

'But maybe they left it too late. Or they didn't persevere. Or they weren't as close together as we two always have been.'

To this there was no reply at all. And he wondered about the truth of what he had said. He didn't feel close to this artificial creature lying on the couch. Of course he and Judith had always believed in people being happy if their minds were compatible, and their thoughts had always been shared: there was no reason why they shouldn't go on as they always had done, for her mind was still active. No reason at all. No reason why he should be conscious of a barrier between them. Yet he could sense that she was not hurrying to agree with him. He even felt that if he did not insist, what he had said so far would drift out of her mind and she would not even bother to reply.

'They've got hold of you already,' he said with abrupt bitterness. 'You've soon forgotten — forgotten everything.'

'It is hard to explain,' she said. 'One feels so different.'

There it was again: that infuriating vagueness. But Warren was not going to be defeated. He settled himself close to the side of the being that he found it so hard to call Judith, and in an undertone outlined his plans. She would listen to all the Greys told her, and report to him when they met. She would try to get herself a responsible job and find out what their long-term plans were. She would, as soon as the opportunity presented itself, visit one of their exclusive clubs and find out what went on there. One thing that he dinned into her over and over again, as if to counteract the weight of the propaganda that would be used against her: 'You're not going to give in to them. You're going to be stubborn. You're going to remember that you are a human being and that your duty is to the human race.'

'Yes,' said the level monotone.

He left her in a mood of bewilderment, not sure whether he had achieved anything — or nothing.

* * *

Warren was sunk in thought as he made his way down the corridor towards the lift. He stepped through the door automatically, paying no attention to the other figure that entered behind him.

It was the sound of a quiet sob that aroused him. He glanced up.

His companion in the smoothly dropping lift was not, as he had assumed, a Grey, but a young woman of about his own age. He said uncomfortably: 'Anything I can do?'

'Nothing,' she said through her tears.

'Someone you're fond of? Ill?'

She nodded, then shook her head. 'He doesn't call it being ill, though. None of them do. He's glad it's happened.'

Warren stared, then light dawned on him. 'You mean someone has gone over to the Greys?'

'My father.'

'Oh! I'm sorry.'

'He's not,' she said with sudden vigour. 'He's not at all sorry. For years he's been longing to reach the end of his ordinary life and go in with the Greys.'

The lift halted, and the doors slid back. The two of them stepped out into the great hall, and instinctively fell into step, walking together across the smooth expanse towards the main entrance. Greys plodded silently about them.

At the top of the steps, Warren hesitated. He could not bear to go off alone into the ordinary everyday world and pretend that nothing had happened. And he sensed the misery and loneliness of the girl who stood beside him. He said: 'Where are you going now?'

'Home, I suppose.'

'Come and have a drink. There's a kafamat over the road.'

'Well . . . '

Her uncertainty was easily overcome. She wanted to talk to someone, just as he did. They could talk at one another, not taking much trouble to listen: an audience, responsive or otherwise, was all that mattered.

They sat at a small table in the window, with the bulk of the hospital overshadowing them. Warren slipped coins in the slots, and in a few seconds the delivery trap opened and they took out their warm drinks. To Warren there was no taste in the liquid. He watched the girl sipping at hers, and knew that she, too, was unaware of flavour or warmth or sweetness. He said abruptly: 'I'm Warren Caldicott.'

'I'm Deborah Quentin.'

He nodded, registering the name and no more; and the echoes came to life, and he looked across the table at her. 'Not Professor Alaric Quentin's daughter?'

She nodded, and gulped. The tears came back into her eyes.

'I see,' said Warren slowly. Then he

added: 'His death is a great blow to all of us. He was one of the best scientists we have ever had. He was the only one who could win respect from the Greys. Now that he's gone — '

'He's glad to be gone!' Deborah burst out. 'All he ever thought of was life in his laboratory. He was a good father to me — in his own way he was affectionate — but he never really cared for anything but research. He wanted to die. He wanted his body to collapse so that he would be taken in with the Greys and given all their facilities. Travel to the planets, infra-atomic research . . . he fretted for the day when he would be one of the Greys.'

'And now he's been taken over.'

'Now,' she nodded wretchedly, 'he has been taken over. I went to see him today, and already he's far away. He's glad to have got away from me. Yes, glad! He doesn't think it's cruel to be so pleased: he just doesn't care any longer. He can't even be bothered to be polite. All that matters now is that he shall be released from the hospital and started on some scientific work.' Her anger faded as quickly as it had come, and she sat staring at the table.

'What will you do now?' said Warren quietly. 'Have you any other family?'

'None. But I'll manage. He left everything very neatly. He's been planning it all for years. Methodical to the end! Oh, yes, I'm well provided for. But' — she faltered — 'I was fond of him. I'll miss him, and I know he won't miss me.' She wiped her eyes angrily, while Warren preserved a sympathetic silence. Then she said: 'I'm a fool to get in such a state about it. I imagine you've got your worries as well.'

He did not need much prompting. In a few minutes he was telling her about Judith. When he had finished, Deborah leaned forward and spontaneously covered his fingers with hers. 'It's worse for you than for me,' she said. 'At least I've known it was coming. But for you to lose her like that . . . '

'I haven't lost her,' said Warren, 'yet.'

Deborah's eyes widened. He saw that they were hazel eyes: bright with tears at the moment, they could be warm and delightful at other times, he was sure. 'I've never heard of any one keeping in touch with a Grey,' said Deborah.

Perhaps he ought not to have spoken. Perhaps, he thought even as he was telling her his plans, he would have been better advised to go on with his scheme secretly. But there was something about her that made it impossible to remain uncommunicative. Briefly he told her what he hoped to do.

There was disbelief in her face. 'It won't work.'

'Oh, yes, it will.' Because he wanted to be sure himself, he went on enthusiastically, expressing his confidence to her and at the same time bolstering up his own belief. He explained how he and Judith had been so close; how they appreciated, really, the ideas of abstract thought; and how they wanted to turn the undoubted powers of the Greys to a better use.

Deborah's expression was puzzling. When he came to the end and waited for her to offer some encouragement she shook her head slowly. 'She must have been an . . . an unusual girl,' she said.

'She was. She had a remarkable mind. If I can keep in contact with her . . . '

Deborah eyed him quizzically. Unexpectedly, she said: 'Did you ever make love to her?'

Warren felt himself flushing. It seemed a monstrous question, and an irrelevant one, too. 'Really,' he said. 'I don't see what that's got to do with it. Anyway, it depends what you mean by . . . well, I don't see it does any good talking about it now.'

There was an uncomfortable pause. At last Deborah said: 'I'm sorry. I had no business to ask such an impertinent question.'

'Oh, that's all right.' But it had left him feeling strangely unsettled. There had been some implication in her question — something sharp and feminine, almost malicious. She was one of those flighty young things; that was the trouble: her mind ran on romance and trivialities instead of on the important things of life. You only had to look at her to see that.

As though to prove it to himself,

Warren looked frankly and searchingly at her. Deborah had fair hair that was drawn back from her brow to reveal the beauty of her high forehead. Even though, in her distress at her father's transformation, she had not taken any pains with her appearance today, nothing could spoil the perfection of her features. Her mouth was small yet sensitive and generous; Warren could not help wondering what she looked like when she smiled.

'I'm sorry,' she said again, getting up. 'It's been so nice to talk to you. I oughtn't to have spoilt it by saying what I did.' He rose, and they went out together. She glanced at him uncertainly as they paused by the moving paveway. 'I hope everything works out all right,' she said.

'I'll let you know.'

'Will you?'

Warren surprised himself by saying: 'Can I see you tomorrow evening? Let me take you out somewhere.'

'Well . . . '

'Or the day after. It'll be the weekend. If we can't be cheerful at least we can share our sorrows.' He spoke lightly, with a deliberate facetiousness, but he found that he was waiting anxiously for her reply.

She studied him gravely, and now her eyes were clear and beautiful. She said: 'All right.'

* * *

The next day he worked like an automaton. For once, the edge of his resentment was dulled. Usually he did the job perfunctorily, studying the records of the Education Bureau and making out a formal report to his departmental director for forwarding to the Grey authorities, all without needing to apply more than half his mind. The other half rehearsed arguments — imaginary arguments with influential Greys, imaginary speeches to a populace ripe for revolution.

But today he did not want to think. He wanted the time to pass quickly so that he could be with Judith again. Resolutely he put speculations out of his mind, and worked hard: so hard that he had done two or three days' work in the space of his four-hour working day.

The time had passed quickly enough. He could relax now and let himself wonder about the coming interview. A faint twitch of dread plucked at his heart. The hospital was, for all its space and lightness, a frightening place.

One of his friends passed him on the way out. 'Going flying this afternoon, Warren?'

'Not this afternoon.'

'You don't get enough exercise. Grab yourself a nice wench, take her to Stellar Park, and begin to live, son!'

Voices chattered about him. A girl came to meet one of the men from the office, and they kissed. Another couple went past arm-in-arm. Somebody laughed, and Warren heard an arch voice saying: 'It's a great world.'

A great world. Only if you didn't think. Only if you had no standards, no values, no essential seriousness of temperament.

Warren scowled at the crowds that came surging out on to the paveways. Many of them were heading for the restaurants in the centre of the city, and after that they would be going on to Stellar Park or the outskirts, where you could fly or go dancing in the floating halls.

He couldn't endure a crowd today. He wanted get to the hospital quickly. He flagged a helicar.

Now that he was on his way, he absurdly felt a desire to put off the moment when he and Judith would meet. He was rushing towards her far too quickly. Within a brief time of leaving the office, he was sitting beside the couch in the hospital. The Grey — he found he could not call it Judith, though he tried to believe that Judith was there — was no longer lying down. It sat up, yet this did not make it look alive: it gave an impression of being a machine that did not spring into action until a human being gave it a reason for reacting. You felt you had to reach out and switch on.

Warren said conventionally: 'Everything going all right? No complications?' As though, he thought, he were asking about an operation for appendicitis.

'I am well. And you?'

'I still don't believe it's happened.'

'It has happened. You may be sure of that.'

Warren leaned forward. 'Tell me what sort of day you've had. What have you learned?'

There was a pause. When Judith began to speak, she did so in a precise voice that made her sentences sound like detached parts of a recitation. She had been taught a formal little lesson, and she was repeating it.

'I have been instructed in the first problems with which new Greys must cope. There are no restrictions. We may meet humans if we wish. We may retain our old friends if we wish.'

'Then why do none of them — none of *you*, that is — do so? What goes wrong?'

'It is better for us not to torment ourselves.'

Warren snorted. 'That's a good one!'

The voice said, without the anguish or melancholy that the words themselves might have implied: 'There is no feeling left, Warren. Warmth means nothing. There is no sense of touch, no smell of flowers. Sound is a technical affair, not a sense: we hear sounds because we must, but they mean nothing. Music means nothing, because the rest of the body is not there to derive pleasure from it.'

'I don't get that at all,' Warren protested. 'Music is the most perfect of the abstract arts. You don't need arms and legs and a torso in order to appreciate Beethoven.'

'Without the human body, something is missing. It can not be explained: it can only be experienced. And all the small sensual pleasures are gone.'

It all came oddly from Judith. Warren was at a loss. Eventually he said: 'But you get used to that in time. It's only a matter of readjustment, isn't it?'

'Readjustment,' the Grey echoed tentatively, without conviction.

'Do you mean to say that's all you've been told? What sort of job are you going to get?'

'I may go to Mars.'

'So that's the game, is it? They want to get you away so that I can't keep tabs on you. Judith, you've got to fight against that. We haven't learnt a thing yet. We've got to find out what goes on in their secret council meetings, and in the clubs — '

'I asked about the clubs.'

Warren caught his breath. Somehow the exclusive Grey clubs epitomised all that he most hated in the overlords. A world that boasted of its freedom, a world that was told over and over again by the Greys themselves that it was a wonderful place where men and women could live as they pleased: what place was there in such a world for buildings which were open only to the dictators? Once upon a time, said the historians, black men had not been allowed in hotels in many countries. There had been a time when Jews were persecuted. There had been houses and clubs in Eastern countries which were barred to men whose colour was not white. All that, said the Greys, had been done away with: yet they maintained those palatial buildings, and no human being had ever been allowed in them. There were tales of orgies, of strange pleasures unknown to the unsophisticated folk of flesh and blood. There, if anywhere, lay the key to the real activities of the Greys. Such a place was a symbol.

Warren said: 'What did you find out?'

'I will not need to go to one yet.'

'What does that mean? It's not a question of needing to go. I mean, you're a Grey now. If you want to walk in — '

'They say that I will not need to go yet. That is all.'

He went on questioning her, without result. It was not so much that her replies were evasive as that their terms of reference were somehow not the same. She seemed to be judging his remarks by new standards that had been insidiously established in her mind.

Not until he got up to go, feeling baffled and frustrated, did she offer a gleam of hope.

'Tomorrow there will be some developments. The classification process, they call it.'

'I'll see you in the evening, then . . . ' Warren stopped abruptly. He remembered now that he had promised to take Deborah Quentin out. He cursed silently.

He would have to get out of that.

But Judith, apparently unaware of his hesitation, said calmly: 'Not tomorrow. You cannot come tomorrow.'

For a moment he wanted to challenge her on this. Then he decided to let it go. Give her a clear day, and she might learn something. If he came back the day after that, she ought to have something to tell him.

'Will you still be here?' he asked.

'I shall be in the Training Wing.'

'I'll call for you there.'

He felt that he ought to take her hand — her cold, artificial hand with its inhuman flexible fingers and its inhuman strength — and tell her to take care of herself, or something sentimental and human like that; but it was silly, and so he said nothing.

When he turned back for a second at the door of the ward, she — *it* — was not even looking in his direction.

* * *

Saturday was a bright day. Weather Control had been able to stabilise a depression, and the tentative promises of a sunny day were to be fulfilled. When Warren met Deborah near the uptown monorail terminus, she was wearing a fresh, sparkling summer dress that lay with crisp attractiveness against the sun-warmed smoothness of her skin. He caught his breath. She was far too attractive. She was the sort of young woman who took your mind off social and political problems: and such women were dangerous.

Deborah smiled at him, her eyes sparkling enticingly. 'Something wrong?'

'Not at all,' he said. Oddly enough, he was conscious of a lightening of his spirits. This, after all, was Saturday, and he could be excused for taking time off from his problems. There was nothing to be done until he had seen Judith again tomorrow. He said: 'Where shall we go?'

'Anywhere you like.'

He said what he had never meant to say: 'Stellar Park?'

She laughed. 'I'd be glad to. I think we need somewhere frivolous.'

On the train he was acutely aware of

her shoulder against his. He wondered guiltily whether he was being disloyal to Judith. But this had nothing to do with that psychic *entente* between himself and Judith. This was a day's forgetfulness, a way of filling in time and no more. It counted for nothing; it was isolated, and would lead to nothing.

He had been to Stellar Park only a few times before, and that had been some years ago, when he had gone along reluctantly with some rowdy friends. Even then he had not enjoyed the noise and excitement and boisterousness of the pleasure grounds. Now, standing beside Deborah, he looked with distaste at the signs glowing in the sky, invisibly strung across the heavens: the enticements of the Sensation Cave, the Underwater Adventure, and all the cheap shows and booths.

'You take life seriously, don't you?' said Deborah gently.

He turned to reply, to repudiate the implied reproach, but the words were snatched from his lips and blown away by a sudden gust of diffused music that seemed to rise from the very ground at their feet. The air throbbed with the latest complex vibrachords, twitching at the nerves and blotting out coherent thought.

In the middle of the uproar he looked into Deborah's eyes and saw sadness welling up in them once more. He realised that her defiant cheerfulness was only a pose: she, like himself, wanted to forget, and had been looking forward to this day as something that would wipe out the past just for a little while.

Warren said quickly: 'Shall we try the Underwater?'

At once she nodded. They made their way through the surging crowds towards the edge of the sea and the gaudy booths shaped like whales and coral reefs. Warren changed quickly in his booth into the sleek trunks and helmet, and fitted the small propulsion unit on his shoulders. Then he went out to the jetty to wait for Deborah. He looked down into the green water that shaded away to deep blue a hundred yards from the shore. It looked cold, yet inviting. And down there it would be quiet. You could listen to music if you wanted to, by switching on the helmet receiver. But he wasn't going to do that. He felt suddenly glad that he had come, and that he had suggested this particular trip. Under the sea, you could shut out the babble of the world and the jarring exuberance of the persistent background noise.

Deborah joined him. Her body was magnificent under the smooth-fitting costume. She stood proudly beside him, and suddenly he laughed — his first carefree laugh in a long while.

There was a faint spluttering inside his helmet as the speaker came to life. Deborah's voice said in his ear: 'Ready?'

'Let's go,' he said.

They went down into the water with a cool, invigorating shock. The small heater unit glowed into life, but on impulse Warren switched it off. The tingling vitality he experienced was something he didn't want spoilt by an artificial heat stabilisation.

Deborah swam down beside him, twisting gracefully like a sleek and beautiful fish. They smiled at one another, their expressions comically blurred through the helmets and the distorting water. Two hundred yards out, as they went down deeper and swam along above the bottom, watching the strange brown and golden fish leaping up from the rocks in a fantastic ballet, he switched on the heater. The world down here was becoming dark and chill. But he sank into it gratefully. His aches and confusions were drawn out of him, and the rhythm of his movement seemed to set up a corresponding, gentle rhythm in his mind.

'What's that over there?' he asked.

'The Quentin grottoes,' Deborah said. 'My father found them and related them to one of his theories about . . . oh about something.' The way in which she sharply finished told him that pain had jabbed at her once more. She kicked swiftly and impatiently forward, and in a moment he was racing after her. In search of forgetfulness, she laughed, and suddenly it was a chase through the winding underwater caverns, sending fish plunging away and drawing a fine flurry of grey material from the bottom, which soon clouded their helmets.

It was like groping around in a fog. Warren slowed down, anxious not to smash his helmet or rip his flesh against the jutting rock formations. He moved cautiously, trying to pick out Deborah from the slowly subsiding cloud. He groped with one hand, and touched her arm. She stood still. The swirling fog dissolved, and now he could see her. She did not move her arm away.

Then, abruptly, her attention was distracted. She looked past him, over his shoulder.

'What is it?' asked Warren, turning quickly in case there was some unexpected menace coming on them from behind. But there was only a motionless grey figure stationed by one of the jutting rocks.

Deborah said tautly: 'One of the Greys. Doing sentry duty, just to make sure no one has an accident on the rocks.'

'Even down here?' Warren swore softly. 'Can't you ever get away from the damned things?'

'It's all part of their public service:

there were one or two accidents down here in the early days, so the Greys had to install one of their watchmen.'

'Any excuse to intrude! Any excuse to watch every human activity!'

The taste of the day seemed to have been ruined. There was something disturbing and uncanny about the Grey — a creature down here at the bottom of the sea without any mask or breathing apparatus. They swam away from it, but the underwater world had lost its charm. Within a few minutes they surfaced and made for the nearby shore.

Noise struck down at them once more. Silence was left behind in the clouded, twilit deeps; here on land there was music and laughter, and a determination to have a good time. The Greys had made all this possible: the Greys had organised the world so that men worked short hours and played long hours; the Greys had provided the leisure and opportunity for new sports, new pastimes, new ways of getting the best out of life.

If, thought Warren yet again, you didn't ask too many questions.

* * *

They sat in one of the open-air restaurants at the farthest edge of Stellar Park. The music was not too aggressive here.

Deborah said: 'It's been a delightful day.'

'I've enjoyed it,' Warren admitted.

'But you're still brooding over something.'

'I can't help it. This sort of thing — all this amusement — it's only a distraction, isn't it?'

'Is it?'

'The Greys like to keep us happy with this sort of thing while they get on with the real business of life.'

Deborah fingered her lip. The early evening shadows fell across her face and gave it an added mystery, and, at the same time, an added melancholy. She said: 'What *is* the real business of life? You don't think their benevolence might be genuine?'

'Do you think so?' he countered, and went on brutally: 'What about your father? Look how he wanted to get in with them. What does it all add up to?'

'I don't know.' She sipped at her drink and looked at him over the edge of the glass. 'I'm not sure that it does any good talking about it.'

'You can't just go on living as though nothing was happening.'

'No.'

But there was something dry and mocking in her tone. He stared at her. He wondered whether, after all, the sensible thing to do was to ignore the Greys. Let them be dictators, if it didn't interfere with ordinary life. Let Judith be swallowed up by them, as all the rest had been swallowed up, so long as he was left to talk to Deborah, to draw closer to Deborah, perhaps eventually to make love to her and share his life with her . . .

There was a cry that came to them above the distant music. Deborah swung round in her seat. Beyond them, along the line of cliffs overlooking the inlet that cut behind the restaurant at this point, a light was flashing. A man struggled on the edge of the cliffs. Two other figures were holding him back — two figures that showed up, as the light grew stronger, as Greys.

The struggle was over in a few seconds. The three went away. Within ten minutes the rumours that buzzed from table to table in the restaurant had solidified: the true story had reached the place, and was being bandied about.

'Trying to commit suicide!' said Deborah, shaking her head. She lifted her hands slightly from the table, as though feeling drops of rain upon them, and turned her face towards the sky. 'Who would want to leave the world on an evening like this?'

Her beauty cast a spell on Warren. But it did not completely entrance him. His stubborn realism asserted itself. He said: 'You see: they're everywhere. A man who wants to finish with life — perhaps for some overwhelming personal reason — isn't allowed to do it. Why? Are they afraid he's deliberately trying to join them? Or are they afraid he'll damage his brain, and be unfit for their ranks?'

'You can never leave the topic alone,

can you?' sighed Deborah.

He felt suddenly contrite. He ordered more wine, they danced, and when he had taken her home through the glowing streets of the city he kissed her — tentatively, in a way that made her chuckle affectionately and say: 'You're rather nice, Warren. I'm quite alarmed when I think how nice you could be if you weren't so serious.'

He thought a lot about her that night after he had left her, and a lot about what she had said. But next day he was thinking about Judith again. He went off in a mood of grim determination to the Training Wing, where she had said she would be.

They told him he could not see her. He argued, and they were polite but firm. 'You're keeping her away from me!' he shouted, losing his temper.

They told him that it was Judith's own wish. She did not wish to see him. He would not believe it. But they remained polite and firm and blankly uncooperative; and he went out into the sunshine swearing that he would find her somehow.

He scowled at Greys who passed him on the steps: someday, somehow, he was going to break their secret world-dictatorial privilege wide open.

* * *

Judith walked past Warren as he went out. She still found it hard to believe that no one would recognise her. She was no more than a few feet from Warren, and all he did was scowl at her.

How long was it going take her to get used to this sensation of impersonality? All the knowledge and emotion and memory that had once been Judith's were still here, but in some bleak way she was detached: she wondered how long it would take to get over that feeling of wanting to reach out and touch, take hold, feel herself in contact with reality.

Touch . . . As she turned at the top of the steps to watch Warren disappearing into the distance, she put her new, artificial fingers against the marble pillar. They were the most perfect, useful, efficient fingers that Grey ingenuity could devise. They were far more sensitive than ordinary human fingers. Their responsiveness was immediate, and a thousand little fibres communicated the most detailed messages to the mind. Yet there was something lacking. Instinctively Judith turned her face up to the sun — and the surface cells told her that it was warm; and she did not blink, and was conscious of no deep, animal satisfaction.

If she had been capable of a sigh, she would have sighed. She turned and went inside, her eyes adjusting at once to the cool, grey interior. Much cooler, said the surface cells, and an automatic adjustment was made to her body temperature control.

An even, unwearying voice was echoing down the corridor as she went towards her Group Instructor's office. She did not recognise the voice, for here all voices were the same, but the sentiments and the force with which they were expressed identified the speaker. Judith stood a few yards away, all her moving parts relaxed, until the exaltation should have died down.

Her Instructor was standing by his door. Facing him, Professor Alaric Quentin finished a fine peroration.

' . . . and I think that the sooner you recommend my trip to Mars, the better. Obviously the possibilities of linked constructive thought are infinite. As you will know, I have done a great deal of research into psychic force patterns — '

'We know all that, professor.'

'Well, then, when can I get started? Ideal conditions at last. Just what I've been waiting for, all these years.'

'My recommendation will be considered along with those of the other Instructors. You will hear of your classification when Control considers the time is ripe.'

'Lot of messing about! Even now there's red tape. I thought I'd be free of all that. A lot of reforms needed here. A great many things to be done.' Quentin plodded off with the mechanical gait of a Grey, infused perhaps with just a suspicion of his own jerky aggressiveness.

Judith advanced towards her Instructor. She said: 'The professor seems to be full of ambitions. He's very happy to be here.'

'So many start out like that,' said the Instructor. 'But in time . . . ' Then he stopped.

'What do you mean?' Instead of replying, the Instructor moved aside and motioned to her to enter the room.

Judith went in, and he followed her. They stood together in the middle of the room. Chairs stood against a wall, but they were rarely used: a Grey experienced no fatigue in standing, and there was no point in making a complicated mechanism for sitting down. One could do so if one wanted, in a series of short, clumsy movements. Judith had noticed that a few sentimentalists, still lamenting the ordinary life they had given up, sometimes made a point of using the chairs as though they wished to retain old habits. It was for such nostalgic beings that the chairs were provided. At this moment she felt, herself, that she wanted to sit down and pretend to be a normal, living woman again; but her pride kept her upright.

The Instructor said: 'You took the first step, then?'

She nodded. 'I did not see him. I sent a message that I did not want to see him.'

'Good. You feel strong about it?'

'No,' said Judith frankly.

'Resignation will come in time.'

'I am not sure that I want to be resigned,' said Judith. She felt weak. If she could have cried, she would have cried. She was angry with herself: but in this body there was no tingling of the flesh, no constriction of the throat, no pounding of blood or stinging of tears. 'I want to go back,' she said. 'I don't want to let go of the world.'

'It is like that for all of us in the early stages. But now you have taken the first step, the rest is not so hard. Perhaps you will be chosen to go to Mars. That is a much bigger break, but somehow you will find it easier. The old ties snap, one by one.'

'Yes,' said Judith. 'I would like that.'

She was not sure if this was true. She was not sure about anything. Warren's face seemed to haunt the depths of her mind. She was conscious of a dreadful loss — not only of what had been, but of the things that had not been and might have existed in due course, if only there had been time. If only she had known more about life while she was living it . . .

She said: 'Isn't Mars getting overcrowded?'

'Certainly not. None of the planets are overcrowded. Do not forget that we who go out there cannot produce children. Even though we may live for a thousand years, we must sooner or later disappear, and then there will be room for those new Greys who come behind us.'

'Yes, but a thousand years is a long time. Human children are born in generations of about twenty-five years.'

'Our solar system is still large. We are still only pioneering on the outer planets. It has all been calculated. Do not be alarmed. There will be room for you on Mars, if you want to join the practical groups. Or there are the thinkers on Venus.'

'I'm no thinker,' said Judith, with what was meant to be a laugh.

'No? I am not sure. You will have to find out for yourself.'

'What shall I do today?'

The Instructor hesitated. Judith wished she knew the meaning of these hesitations and the declarations that often followed them. In this cold world, faces gave nothing away. There were no betraying expressions, no human intonations, and no nervous gestures.

Then the Instructor said: 'According to your grading, you should profit from a study of the Community Centre organisation. Report to me when you have been there an hour.'

'But I've never felt any — '

'There is a system in all we do. Please consider it in great detail and report back.'

It was not a command. But you did what was suggested to you in this strange world, this twilight world; you did it because you wanted guidance, and grasped at whatever was offered.

Judith went off. The Instructor, who had been here for two hundred years now, made a methodical note and then sat back. If he had any feelings or regrets, nobody now would ever catch a glimmering of them.

The weeks went by. There were lectures, and there were training courses. Judith realised that, although she was not being regimented in any way, she was being carefully guided. Her aptitudes had been studied, and appropriate steps were being taken. The only thing was, she herself didn't know the direction in which she was being steered.

She did several jobs of work. It was not merely a matter of going to school. She played her part in the community, but at the same time she had the feeling that this was only a training period. She was on probation. Sooner or later — her Instructor would give no indication of when it might be — she would be told what her job was to be for the next thousand years.

There were other people. It could not be said that she was forbidden to make friends: but somehow one did not make friends. The meaning of the word had altered, or it had ceased entirely to have meaning at all. One had colleagues, associates, workmates . . . but not friends.

This was something she had not expected. It did not fit in with the ideas and theories she and Warren had so often exchanged. They had visualised an autocratic society which lived on the best that was to be had. An intellectual aristocracy, arrogant and steeped in luxury: that was how the Greys were regarded. But now she was faced with an austerity that was almost terrifying. She knew, as no flesh and blood human being could know, the deprivation that was experienced when one had lost all the human attributes. There could be no luxury and no debauchery for creatures who worked like machines: the mind could derive no sensual gratification from artificial reflexes and clicking of relays.

What was there to live for?

It was a terrifying question. Human beings might ask themselves that, but it was only rarely that the question became desperate. Something would come along that made them forget the whole thing. They did not pursue it. Forgetfulness came easily. But now there was no forgetfulness: the mind was appallingly clear.

Judith went to her Instructor with the question. 'Where will all this lead? What will make the next thousand years tolerable?'

His answer seemed almost a mockery. 'You are not satisfied with the prospect of abstract thought?'

'No. How could I be? What human being ever could be?'

'Or the joy of serving your fellow beings? Of making the world easier for creatures of the kind that you once were?'

'They don't appreciate it,' said Judith in anguish. 'I know they don't. I never did while I was alive. Some folk get along all right without worrying, but they're the insensitive ones. The others don't like what they call the Grey dictatorship. They spend half their lives fretting, saying how wonderful it is to be a Grey. And *this* is what it is like. Why aren't they told? Why don't you tell them there's nothing to be envious of?'

'Would they believe such a story?'

'If you were convincing enough. If you

showed them — somehow.'

The Instructor's silence was, this time, a sceptical one. At last he said: 'It has been tried. In various ways we have tried to explain to human beings that ours is a life of pure reason and that they should make the most of their own life while it lasts. You must have seen our proclamations yourself. Did you believe them?'

'No,' Judith admitted.

'The insensitive ones paid no heed. They did not mind. We made life comfortable for them, and they indulged themselves without worrying. The sensitive ones continued to resent us, believing that we were trying to keep good things to ourselves. Only once or twice did we convince anyone of the state of affairs in our existence. And that was the worst of all. In comparatively early times, there was a revolt against our growing power. We knew that an uprising was scheduled to take place. We talked to the ringleaders, who were all intelligent men — scientists, idealists, thinkers of the first grade — and showed them just what life here was like. We convinced them. We convinced them too well: a large number of them committed suicide in such a way that their brains were irrecoverable. Others simply disappeared. They didn't want to join us when their bodies died!'

'And if you made every one see what it was like — '

'Then we should lose all the highly developed minds. Only the unthinking, the heedless, the unintelligent, would be available. Our work for the human race would be hampered enormously. For their own good we keep ourselves aloof and secretive. We do their work for them, watch over them . . . '

'And still,' said Judith, 'they will never be happy.'

'We must just do what we can. Things are better than they were five hundred years ago. They continue to improve.'

'Materially, yes,' said Judith. 'But in what other way? If men lose their initiative and leave their destinies in the hands of disembodied brains that have really ceased to be human, what dignity is left to the human race? Is material comfort enough?'

There was another pause. It was as though the Instructor were turning over what she had said; but it could hardly be because the idea was new to him. He said: 'You wonder about that, do you?'

'Of course I do. It all comes back to the same thing: what makes life — our sort of life, as we are now — worth living?'

She received no answer. To her surprise, the Instructor asked her to report for a lecture on Venusian colony conditions the next day.

In a mood of indecision, with a prickling of fear in her mind that might have led her to scream if her throat and mouth had been human, she went out for the rest of the day. She went and watched Warren's office building until he emerged. She followed him. Men and women stood aside to let her pass: some indifferent, some curious, but most of them with envious, resentful faces.

Judith followed Warren when he took Deborah out. She remained unwearyingly close to them, unobserved, undistinguished from the other Greys who went to and fro. And in the evening, her eyes adjusting automatically to the twilight, she watched as Warren kissed Deborah.

Judith studied them. Part of her was detached and analytical. She watched Deborah's arm moving around Warren's shoulder, and the pressure of Deborah's fingers on Warren's back. She saw their eyes closing, and marked the limpness of their bodies as they rested in a close embrace.

And another part of her was crying out with anguish. Warren had never kissed her, Judith, like that. This was something she had never known. And now it was too late. A foolish, simple human affection that meant nothing in the cosmic scheme of things — a minor animal pleasure that could be discarded by a mind capable of abstract thought . . . but she yearned for it as she never yearned for it while she was alive and foolish.

Too late.

* * *

Walking back towards the monorail stop, the two of them saw the Grey standing motionless near a group of drunks who were singing bawdy songs at the Greys.

'Another policeman snooping!' said Warren.

'It's not doing any harm,' said Deborah, her arm linked in his. She brushed her head against his shoulder.

They went past the Grey, who watched them go.

Warren kissed Deborah once more before they reached the station, and then looked back.

Deborah said: 'What's wrong?'

'Nothing. Nothing, I suppose. But . . . '

'Well?'

'I ought to make another attempt to get in touch with Judith.'

'I thought you'd forgotten her?' said Deborah, with a touch of asperity.

'I ought not to have given up so easily.'

'Are you getting bored with me?'

He looked down into the perfection of her face as they stood on the brightness of the platform. 'You know I'm not. But it makes me feel rather ashamed — getting so much out of life that I've just let go of Judith.'

'She wouldn't see you, would she? She didn't want to. That's enough, surely?'

'That was the message I got. But how do I know it's true?'

They did not say much as the train sped back towards the city. But when they approached Deborah's home, he was impelled to say: 'How do you feel about your father? Don't you ever . . . well, wonder?'

'He's forgotten me,' she said, 'and glad to do it. I'm trying to forget him. I've just put up a wall. I don't intend to fret about it.'

Warren shook his head. When they parted, he knew that Deborah was annoyed by his abstraction; but once he had begun to think about Judith, he could not put her out of his mind. The viewpoint had imperceptibly altered: originally he had planned on receiving information from her so that he could understand what the Greys were up to; now his feeling was, incongruously, one of responsibility towards her. The message he had been given was almost certainly a fake. Judith had been trapped by the

Greys and not allowed to communicate with him. Or else she had been lured into accepting their values. He must save her.

It was a fine, noble, defiant thing to say. But it was not so easy to know where to begin.

Warren visited the hospital and the Training Wing. He was treated with cold courtesy, and all his resentment against the Greys came boiling up again. He was ashamed of himself for having let his growing devotion to Deborah take up so much of his time. That was what the Greys had always counted on — the human desire for an easy, uncomplicated life, the love of pleasure.

'I wish to see Judith Carmichael. There's nothing wrong in that, is there? If you're keeping her prisoner for any reason — '

'Why should we keep her prisoner? She is one of us.'

'All I know is that we agreed to keep in touch, now you won't let her see me.'

'Has she expressed the wish to see you?'

Warren stormed at them. They remained

unmoved. He could not understand how he had come to let his hatred fall into abeyance under Deborah's influence. The power of these arrogant machines must be broken. Machines: that was all they were. He must save Judith from such a fate, and use her in his campaign. He said: 'Can you take a message for her? If there aren't any restrictions — and you say there aren't — is there any reason why you shouldn't deliver a message to her and say that I want to see her?'

'If she is available, we can pass it on.'

'Available?' he echoed.

'She may have gone to another planet. Her work may make a meeting between you impracticable.'

'Well, deliver the message, anyway.' He left word that he *wished* to see Judith. He would call here daily for a reply; or she could get in touch with him in any way she chose.

It seemed feeble, but he could think of nothing else to do. He went past great tiers of offices, loathing the Greys who ran everything so efficiently; he passed Greys in the street, and wondered what awful things happened to ordinary human minds to turn them into such cold, unloving machines.

Once more the sight of the entrances to those exclusive clubs enraged him. The stories and rumours added up again — to what? The inner rooms that gossip spoke of. Gaming rooms, secret conference rooms, places of debauchery on a scale unknown to normal human beings . . .

'What does it matter?' said Deborah. It was their first quarrel, and her distress was genuine. 'There's something wrong — abnormal — about your interest in someone who's died.'

'She hasn't died. It isn't the same thing at all.'

'As far as we're concerned, it is,' snapped Deborah. 'All this worrying about what happens — it doesn't help. Can't you take it for granted that there are two races now? If life is all right for us, what does it matter what the Greys do? We can live and be happy; we're not persecuted; nobody interferes with us.'

'That's a dangerous attitude. Besides, what is the point of the secrecy? It's suspicious, you've got to admit that. What's it like to be a Grey? Why don't they tell us?'

Deborah pushed back her hair with one impetuous hand. She made a wild, bewildered gesture. 'How can we tell? There are some questions that you can't expect to be answered. You can't explain to a two-year-old how an atomic motor works. He has to wait until he's at a stage to understand that sort of thing. Maybe it's the same for us, in this connection. And what does it matter? Once upon a time people worried about life after death, and it did them no good, because there was no way of finding out what it was like, without dying. Today we're not so worried, because we know when our bodies die we've got another thousand years or so to go.'

The remark struck a query in Warren's mind. It had never occurred to him before to wonder what the Greys thought about life after death. It was a strange speculation. It was one of those abstractions that could give rise to a stimulating argument. He looked at Deborah, and suddenly cursed himself for being such an awkward character. She was unhappy. She got no pleasure from arguments and abstractions.

He took her arm, and she forced a smile. They said no more about Judith or about the Greys that evening. But Warren had not abandoned his intention of trying to get in touch with Judith.

* * *

I want, thought Judith desperately, at least to be able to dream. I want my mind to stop being clear for a while: I want it to be hazed by daydreams. I want to relax, to pretend that the sun is shining and I am lying on a beach, and Warren is beside me, and he touches my arm as he has touched that other woman's arm, and I want the taste of strawberries and the clear, cool breeze on my cheek and the sights and smells and sounds and all the feelings, and love and laughter, and, oh, why didn't I know what life was while I was still alive?

I want. I want.

Her Instructor said in his dispassionate voice:

'I am sorry to learn that you propose to answer this message the man has left for you. I had hoped you would have been able to overcome such impulses.'

'There's no reason why I shouldn't see him. It doesn't mean anything.'

'If it means nothing, why see him?'

'I shall go on being restless unless I do. Perhaps if I keep in touch with him, things will be better. I shall gradually get better. We shall drift away, and that will be the best way.'

'It has rarely worked like that in the past. That's why we discourage it.'

'But you don't forbid it?'

'We do not forbid it. How could we plead any justification for so doing? You are new to our existence, but you are nevertheless our equal. All Greys are equal. The only laws are those that are instinctively recognised by each and every one of us.'

'In that case I will do this my own way,' said Judith.

'Until you have freed yourself from

such an obsession,' said the Instructor, 'you will be a ghost — an earthbound ghost, wandering between two worlds.' The severity of the criticism was like a physical blow; but it was the nearest the Instructor would ever come to any attempt to coerce her.

As she was about to leave, he spoke suddenly: 'A moment. Wait.'

Judith turned.

'Will you try one thing more first?'

'What sort of thing?'

'A way of forgetfulness. A substitute. You are not the only one who has yearned for the world left behind. In some cases it gets worse as time goes on. And then we offer the Panacea. Before you go on with your own idea, please try this.'

Curiosity, if nothing else, led her to accept the suggestion. But she was still thinking of Warren as they approached one of the large buildings near Saturn Square. Indeed, it made her think even more acutely of Warren, for here at last she was approaching one of those mysterious gathering-places of the Greys which had so incensed him.

They went in and crossed a solemn, imposing foyer. To their right was an open door, and inside it a discussion was going on. The voice of Professor Quentin rose above the general buzz of conversation. 'It's disgusting, the way some of you slip back into that sort of make-believe. Here we are with the universe in our grasp, and you keep harking back like a lot of sentimental women to the past — dreaming yourselves back into that slovenly, hopeless world . . . '

The voice faded away behind them. They passed a group of Greys walking rather unsteadily. If Judith had had a human back, she would have felt a prickle of unease down it. Absurd thoughts flitted through her consciousness: thoughts of opium dens, of the sensual stimulants of the fairground booths in some of the more disreputable provincial cities. Surely the Instructor was not proposing that she should drug or drink herself into insensibility?

Then she realised that drugs and alcohol would have no effect on her. Except to rust her internal workings, perhaps.

A door opened before them. They went into a long corridor, on each side of which were small cubicles. The silence was a strange silence: utter stillness that was somehow loud and overpowering. Judith sensed that most of the cubicles were occupied. It was as though the people in them were thinking, concentrating . . .

Without a word, the Instructor led her into one. She lay on a couch as though in hospital. A pair of anodes were clamped to her head. 'Today you may have twenty minutes,' said the Instructor. 'You may not wish more. Later, the decision will be your own.' He left her, and the door closed.

A pulse began to beat through her mind. The walls of the cubicle receded, then contracted, then receded again, and this time went far, far away. She felt sunshine warm upon her. She lay on a beach, feeling sand between her toes. When she dug her fingers down, they reached colder, damper sand, and the wetness of it was a cool benediction on her flesh.

Warren laughed beside her. She turned to look up at him, and he put his hand on her arm. The grip of his fingers was savage and exciting.

She said: 'Why did you take so long?'

'Do you love me?' he said.

Their mouths met and parted. The breeze blew cool and refreshing; and then they were swimming, the water was cold and exhilarating, and she tasted salt on her lips.

For a space of time that in her imagination was measured in hours, yet seemed to be over in a flash, and was in reality of twenty minutes' duration exactly, Judith lived in the true world — the world she had neglected while she actually belonged to it.

Her awakening was a wretched one. The walls of the cubicle came rushing back, the door opened, and her Instructor came in. She stared at him with hatred: but of course the hatred did not show. Mobility of face and responsiveness of body had been left behind in that dream world. Only mental agony remained.

He said: 'Did you find that everything

went as you would have wished it?'

She got up. 'I feel unclean,' she said. 'I feel as though I have done something immoral — something cheap and perverse.'

'I see. Some people do feel like that. But this is better than trying hopelessly to cling to the past by maintaining relationships with actual people. It is the best solace we can offer until you have completely broken away from the old world.'

Judith said: 'I shall not come here again.'

'The decision is your own, of course. This Panacea is designed only for those who cannot do without it.'

'I shall see Warren, as I planned,' said Judith.

'I am sorry to hear it. You will regret it. It will do neither of you any good.'

Judith walked stiffly out without replying.

* * *

They met in the dunes beyond the city, with the blue sea gleaming before them.

There was nobody near. To the north, men and women on skis were skating out across the gently undulating surface, but the sound of their voices was very faint. They were no more than flecks of colour on the dazzling water.

Warren said: 'I thought I'd never be able to find you again.'

'I did not mean you to do so. Not at first, that is.'

'So it was true what they told me: you really didn't want to see me?'

'I did my best to cut myself off because I believed it was best.'

Warren looked at the emotionless face, and found it incredibly alien. He shivered. He had somehow not expected to feel so remote. He said: 'What have you learnt? You're still in favour of breaking the power of the Greys, I suppose?'

'I have learnt,' said Judith slowly, 'that the Greys derive no pleasure and no advantage from the exercise of power — '

'Now, wait a minute.' So she had been subjected to propaganda: that was what it was; he had suspected she might succumb!

'I have learnt,' she went on inexorably, 'that the life of the mind is not the beautiful thing philosophers have claimed. To be divorced from the body is not a wonderful advantage. I have learnt that the sun and the wind and human love are far more important and mean more to the mind than all the philosophical speculations and theories.'

Warren gaped. He thought suddenly of Deborah, and she seemed very real. Judith, here before him, was unreal.

Suddenly her words quickened. While the voice was still mechanical, produced by a thousand little vibrations of a delicate, finely-mounted diaphragm within the letter box mouth, it became swifter and more urgent. She said: 'Why did you never talk to me the way you talk to that Deborah woman, Warren?'

'What do you know about Deborah?'

'I know that you've held her in your arms and murmured in her ear, saying things you never said to me. I know now that I never even began to live. You persuaded me that we were kindred spirits — that was your phrase, wasn't it?

— and so we were above all the sentimental nonsense that other young couples indulged in. And I believed you. I thought so much of you that I was sure you must be right. Books and literatapes and generalisations were all that we ever shared.'

'But you weren't the sort of girl who — '

'How did you know what sort of girl I was? Did you ever try to find out anything about me? You took it for granted that I wanted only to listen to you and encourage you in your petty grumblings against the Greys. I never had the chance of learning how sweet life could be. But you haven't been so dispassionate with this Deborah, have you? Now that it's too late, I know what I might have been to you. Now that it's too late.'

Warren felt a cold dread. This was something he had never expected. The thought that a machine could frame such remarks, driving them home with such force, was a terrifying, unnatural one. He licked his lips and thrust his hands down into the warm sand as though to push himself up and escape. He said: 'Things are different. I mean . . . well, life goes on, you know. If I'd realised . . . But there's nothing to be done now, is there?' There was a pause. She did not reply . . .

'Is there?' he said again.

Judith moved towards him. The machine was ungraceful, but in some way horribly purposeful. The metallic voice said: 'I'm lonely, Warren. You can't understand the meaning of this loneliness. If I can't have you as a human being, as Deborah is having you — talking and laughing with her, touching her arm, making love to her — if I can't have that, at least I have a claim to your mind.'

'Of course you have. We always got on well together. We always had plenty to say to one another,' said Warren desperately, wildly.

'I think you should join me.'

'I don't know what you mean.'

'Perhaps this world will be less lonely if you're in it with me.'

Warren tried to cry out, but the flexible, strong fingers were at his throat. He lashed out, and bruised his fists against the unyielding body. They went down in the sand together, and with remorseless fingers tightening in a grip that could not be broken. The blue of the sea and sky was shot through with vicious colours before Warren's eyes. Vainly he hammered against the metal, feeling himself growing weaker, with a pounding in his head that threatened to split it open.

'Come with me,' said Judith. 'You must come.'

Then the pressure relaxed. There was another figure there — a Grey who prised Judith's fingers open and pulled her back.

Warren lay where he was for a moment, fighting for breath. His throat ached. He tried to push himself upright, and fell back. The two Greys stood over him, one restraining the other. He could see little difference between them.

One of them spoke, and something in the spacing of the phrases told him that it was not Judith. 'You have been told what our life is like. Perhaps you will realise now that we are not to be envied. Your time will come soon enough — don't try to find out too much now. Go back and live.'

And then Judith spoke. There was no regret in that voice which could express neither happiness nor regret. She said: 'Yes, Warren. I am sorry. You see what madness can possess us. Go back . . . and don't waste life. There isn't much of it.'

Then she and the Grey who had come to Warren's rescue turned and stalked off. They lumbered over the sand dunes, leaving him to struggle to his feet and make his way home.

He was weak and enervated. It had all been a nightmare. He had a vision of the Greys living in a cold, sterile limbo — into which he himself would one day be drawn. The terror came over him in an icy wave. He started away from a Grey he passed in the street, and looked at the unconcerned faces of the human beings who milled around him.

A week later he and Deborah were married.

* * *

The Instructor said nothing to Judith. She waited for condemnation or criticism, but there was no open comment. The silence weighed down on her. She sensed reproof, and wished that it could be spoken.

In the end it was she who broached the subject. 'My attempt to kill Warren . . . What are you going to do about it?'

'The attempt did not succeed. Such attempts are never allowed to succeed.'

'You mean there have been others? The same sort of thing has happened before?'

'Frequently. We are prepared for such mistakes.'

'I don't know how I could have been so foolish. It was madness. I don't know what I'm going to do.'

'You would care to visit the Panacea, possibly?'

'No,' snapped Judith. 'That hideous pretence — it's degrading.'

'The pretence is all we can offer. If you long for the life of the senses, the physical existence of your human frame, there is no other substitute.'

'I must turn my back on all that.'

There was one of those pauses fraught with meaning. Then the Instructor said: 'What do you want to do?'

'There's no such thing as 'I want' any longer,' said Judith. 'I just want forgetfulness — or to be told what to do. There doesn't seem any way out. Nothing that I think or recall from that other life applies any more. If only there could be darkness . . . ' She hesitated, then went on: 'Why do the Greys go on? If existence is misery for all of us, why don't we give up? We could let ourselves die — turn off the power, let our robot bodies run down. Then human beings wouldn't feel resentful any longer, and we would know peace.'

'It is a question we all come to.'

'And the answer?'

'There are different answers. Let me tell you what you have not so far been told. If you wish to end your life now, you may do so. There is no restriction. We do not forbid suicide, though we deplore it.'

Judith felt a surge of relief. It would be so easy. The idea of that beautiful, endless sleep, waiting for her as soon as she chose to accept it, was a warm promise. She said: 'And a good many Greys do finish like that?'

'A certain number.'

'What about the others? What makes existence tolerable for them?'

'There are different answers,' said the Instructor again. 'You have been told, before you came here as well as since you joined us, that the Greys work for the good of mankind. Terrestrial and interplanetary administration is in the hands of the Greys. We work on other planets in conditions that no human being could survive. We are the organisers and, one might say, the guardian angels. There is nothing in what we do that gives us any personal gratification — '

'But why go on doing it? Human beings don't want it. They are full of suspicion. They would be glad if the Greys were wiped out. And it might do them good: it would renew human initiative.'

'Would it? It might renew old jealousies and lead to new wars. You cannot repudiate scientific progress, even when it takes a wrong turning: and we don't know yet whether this is a wrong turning or not. All we know is that this thing has happened, and we must cope with it. We must *cope*. If we scrapped ourselves now, there would still be resentments. The more sensitive men might be persuaded to understand. But the others — the vast majority — would be furious. They would hate us for destroying the secrets of those thousand years that are now promised to every man when his body ceases to function. And in a generation or two, even the intelligent ones would have forgotten. They would strive to rediscover the secret. And in due course they would do so. They would have to start all over again, making the mistakes that our earliest members made, painfully learning from experience and rebuilding our interplanetary empire. And in the meantime? The problems of the overcrowded world would have to be dealt with by human beings rather than by ourselves. It would be a hopeless retrogression. Things may be imperfect now, but we cannot turn back: we must struggle through, and see what is waiting on the other side.'

'It's a pity this unnatural system of prolongation of the mental life was ever thought of.'

'There were those,' said the Instructor, 'who lamented the invention of the aeroplane. Possibly they were right. But once it had been invented, it could not be repudiated. When men have brought about a change, they must deal with the consequences of the change, not try to rub it out and act as though it had never been.'

Judith felt lost. The momentary illusion of comfort was fading rapidly.

'But,' she ventured, clutching at a strand of hope, 'you say it is all right if any of us wish to . . . to play no further part? We can die?'

'You are allowed to die,' conceded the Instructor. 'But what will happen then? What lies beyond death?'

She stared. The two faces regarded one another, and saw what might have been reflections in a mirror.

'I don't understand,' said Judith. 'You're not suggesting . . . ?' The words failed to come. She could not deal with concepts that were unfamiliar to minds of her century.

'I suggest nothing. Anything I said to you would sound old-fashioned. This is a subject on which we make no declarations. We do not give lectures on it. It is something you must find out for yourself, if you wish to find it.'

Judith hesitated. Then she said: 'You think I should go to Mars? Just go on working for the benefit of the human race . . . waiting until I can die in the ordinary course of events?'

'You can stay on Earth if you wish. There are useful jobs here. When things become too overpowering, you can resort, as so many of us do, to the Panacea — '

'No!'

'Or you can join the colony on Venus.'

She sensed some meaning in this that was more intense than anything which had yet been said to her.

'You've never told me exactly what the Venusian group do.'

'Because we down here are not sure. We do not know what they are really searching for, or how close they have got to it. All we can say is that they lead a monastic life, seeking, perhaps trying to find the same answers that we are all seeking; and perhaps taking a more promising road than the one that we are on.'

'You mean . . . a religious order?'

'Religion? I cannot say. Not what our ancestors would have understood by that word. Something beyond.'

'But what can there be? The human race gave up the worship of supernatural beings centuries ago.'

'That could have been a mistake. Just as we are superior in many ways to the human race, so there may be something superior to ourselves. We work for human beings, although our capabilities are greater than theirs. And when we ourselves die, there is no telling what work still lies ahead. Some of us work in a practical way now; the Venusians are reaching outwards, upwards — and theirs may be the right answer in the end.'

'You can't tell me more than that?'

'No more than that,' said the Instructor.

Judith spent several days considering the detailed reports available on the Martian settlements. She studied in the terrestrial administration offices, along with several newcomers to the Greys who fancied the idea of administrative posts. Once she went to the Panacea, but hesitated on the steps and then turned away.

In the end she came back to her Instructor and said: 'I will go to Venus.'

The brief nod of the head was formal and unsurprised. 'We were sure from the very beginning that that was where your interests lay.'

'But I've never had any idea — '

'It was clear to us. We do not often make mistakes. But we must let each mind make its own discoveries.'

'If I'm wrong? If I want to come back?'

'Then you may come back. But you are not wrong. I envy you. I wish you peace and fulfilment: and may you find the answer.'

* * *

Warren and Deborah were happy for some years, and then reasonably contented. Time blurred the first passion, and blurred many other things. At first his feelings about the Greys were completely submerged: when they stirred in the back of his mind, he repulsed them. The horror of Judith's attack, and the threat that lay behind it, gave him an occasional nightmare. But life was vigorous, and in the daylight his uneasy memories were blown away.

It was Deborah who first prodded his old resentments into wakefulness. 'When,' she demanded, 'are you going to get a promotion? You've been in that office long enough, goodness knows.'

'I don't see how I can get any higher. All the higher-grade posts are filled by Greys.'

'The Greys are getting their hands on everything nowadays. Haven't you got any courage at all? When is someone going to do some thing about it?'

'Well . . . there's a new party being formed to try to counteract the Grey influence in the World Council. But I don't know if it'll come to anything.'

'It certainly won't, if folk like you sit about doing nothing. I wish I knew what the Greys were up to. If I were a man, I'd want to break their power once and for all. If you had any pride . . . '

He remembered Judith, and all that Judith had implied about her twilight world. Yet now it did not seem so frightening. It did not even seem true. How could he be sure that it wasn't all nonsense? The Greys were always handing out propaganda designed to soothe people and keep them from rebelling.

He wondered whether to tell Deborah what Judith had told him — he had never mentioned it to her — and then realised how absurd it would sound. Of course it was absurd. He must have been a fool ever to have believed it, even for a moment. He had been a coward.

The sight of a Grey in the street became once more a source of bitterness. He joined the Human Rights Association, and became one of their most virulent campaigners. Anger at his own gullibility drove him on to more and more vigorous attacks on the Grey overlords.

He was one of the leaders in the armed uprising that took place on the first day of the great Interplanetary Conference in the metropolis. It was put down without much trouble by the Greys, and the only casualties were those men who, in the struggle on the steps, fell and were trampled to death.

Warren was one of the victims. As death came to him, he thought, with a strange mixture of panic and exultation: Now I shall know. Now I'll see what these dictators are like, and what sort of autocratic lives they lead. But I won't be like the rest of them. I'll be loyal to the human race. No inducement will tempt me to be really one of them. Nothing. Now I shall see . . .

THE LOST CHILD

At first she tried to pretend that it was the wind. Or perhaps it was merely the uneasy whimper a child makes when turning over in its sleep. She stirred the cocoa slowly in the pan, leaning her forehead against the low mantelpiece and willing herself to hear nothing out of the ordinary. There had been no sound: it was her imagination, could be nothing else.

But she was still listening. Despite the warmth of the fire prickling in her cheeks she felt a chill down her back. No, not again. She couldn't go through it again . . .

It was not the wind. It came, faint and unmistakable, from the room above.

Mrs. Neal took the pan away from the fire and waited for her knees to stop trembling. The cry might be an ordinary one — fear of the dark, wanting a drink, or just calling out for the sake of calling out — and then she would have only to utter a few reassuring words. She would watch with pleasure Janet's sleepy smile, always so elusive and fascinating when the light of the candle chased it into the shadows at the corner of her mouth. And for a moment there would be the drowsiness of Janet's voice. The kitchen was always too quiet after Janet had gone to bed; the silence was like a curtain draped about the room, with no one to disturb its thick, oppressive folds.

Once there had been Hugh, his legs stretched out towards the fire, his lazy voice chasing away the mists of loneliness that seemed to creep out of the very walls of this cottage, standing solitary upon its bleak hillside. Once there had been Hugh; but no more. Hugh would not have been frightened by a little girl's dream. Hugh would have gone upstairs without hesitation instead of fingering the handle of the pan and pretending that it might not be necessary after all to light the candle and go up the creaking stairs.

For a third time she heard the cry.

She took the oil lamp from the table. On each of the past three evenings she had taken the candle so that its flickering light would not glare into Janet's eyes. But tonight she was scared. Tonight she would carry the defiant brightness of the lamp into that bedroom.

The wind from the moors whispered along the hillside and in through the ill-fitting back door, chasing her with mocking gusts up the stairs.

Janet's voice was clear now. 'Mummy, where are you? Come a bit nearer, please.'

Mrs. Neal opened the door. Tonight the feeling of enmity was stronger. It was something tangible, lurking beyond the radiance of the lamp. It jeered at her as she set the lamp down on the dressing-table beside the photograph of Hugh in uniform. He smiled out at her but was incapable of offering any reassurance.

Janet dragged her arms out from under the sheet. 'Mummy, it's coming again. Stop it, or I'll be lost again. Lost . . . Don't let it, Mummy.' Her eyelids were closed but trembling. Just as they had been on Christmas Eve when she was pretending to sleep, thought her mother. The happy comparison was incongruous:

in this bedroom now there was nothing but terror.

'I'm here, Janet,' she said quietly. She sat on the edge of the bed and took hold of one of the clutching, aimless hands.

'Mummy, it's here again. It wants me. It's after me. Stop it — do something before it's too late and I've slipped away again. Oh, *please* . . . ' The appeal ended in a whimper of anguish.

Mrs. Neal said: 'Janet, darling, I'm here.'

The hand freed itself from her grasp and waved her away. She seized it again as though she herself needed support. 'Jan — '

The child frowned and muttered. 'It's no good, Mummy. It's still too strong. I'm going . . . going. But I'll be back soon. When you call me loud enough. You must make it very loud. I can't hold on now.'

'You're all right,' said the woman desperately. She was sobbing in the back of her throat because she did not know what she was fighting or why she had to fight. 'You're not going anywhere, Jan. You're with me. You're safe.'

'Going . . . '

Janet's eyes opened. The lamp glittered in them so that at first it looked as though she had been blinded by tears. Then the film was wiped away. Her mouth twisted in the slight smile that was so breathtakingly like Hugh's smile. She said: 'Hello, Mummy.'

Mrs. Neal drew a deep breath. She had got her daughter back. They had been separated and were reunited. It was for the fourth time.

The fourth time. This would have to be stopped somehow.

She must tread warily so that Janet would not be frightened. 'Jan, darling . . . ' But how to begin?

'Talking in my sleep again?' said Janet in a small voice.

'Yes, you certainly were.' She forced a laugh and tried to sound casual. 'What were you dreaming about this time?'

Her daughter turned her dark head on the pillow and stared at the wall. She began to trace wavering outlines in the air with one finger. 'The same as last night, I think. And other nights, too. But I'm not sure. I jus' think so, that's all.'

'Not many people dream the same dream four nights running.'

'Don't they?'

'What a queer little girl you are, aren't you?'

'I don't know.'

'You were talking about going away. Who were you going away from? Or can't you remember?' Fear leapt from the shadows beyond the lamp like a sly cat.

'Can't 'member much. But I was leaving Mummy. I was being pulled away from my Mummy.'

'Well, it didn't come true, did it? I'm here, and you're still here.'

Janet rolled over on her back. She looked puzzled. 'That's right.' But she was doubtful. 'You're here and I'm here. But . . . ' She could find no words.

'Well,' said her mother briskly, 'you've no business to be awake and talking at this time of night, anyway. I'll tuck you up again and then we'll have some sleep, shall we — without any dreams.'

Without any dreams. She prayed for that on the way downstairs. She could not conceive what would happen if this went on. Each time it was becoming harder to recall Janet from the strange world into which she had wandered: in four nights she seemed to have penetrated deeper and deeper into it, getting further away from any voice that tried to call her back. Mrs. Neal felt there would come a time — perhaps soon, too soon — when the two of them would lose touch with each other altogether. She was in a dream herself, a dream in which she ran without moving and reached out with her arms towards an eight-year-old girl who grew smaller and smaller as she was dragged into the distance.

* * *

At breakfast next morning she waited for Janet to say something. Janet, however, finished her milk without mentioning the dreams. It was not until the end of the meal that, as though recalling something which perplexed her, she looked about the small room with a questioning tilt of her head and asked suddenly: 'This *is* home, isn't it?'

'Of course it is, chick.'

'I was just wondering. I thought there was something funny.' Then she seemed to accept everything as abruptly as she had questioned it, and there was nothing unusual in her expression as she grinned across the table. 'I'd better hurry, hadn't I?'

Mrs. Neal made her decision. It was a decision she had contemplated in the middle of the night as she lay awake and from which she had backed away in the cold, welcome light of morning. She returned to it now because in one blinding second she had visualised what it would be like when evening came again, when the curtains were drawn and she stood by the fire making supper, or sat reading and sewing, not daring to switch on the harsh old radio in the corner in case its tinny voice drowned the noise she dreaded to hear but could not ignore. Not another evening like that; no more evenings like that!

She said: 'You're not going to school

this morning. We're going to see the doctor.'

'Why? What do I have to go to the doctor's for? I don't feel poorly.'

'I'm sure there's something wrong with . . . with your inside. All those funny dreams. It must be bad digestion or something.'

'But I don't have a tummy-ache.'

'I've had enough of running upstairs and lying awake,' said her mother crisply, 'wondering if you're going to call out.'

Janet said: 'I'm all right, really. I mean, I don't *mind* the dreams.'

'Don't mind them? But you're always struggling and thrashing about, and crying about going away and leaving me.'

'I don't think so. Not really, Mummy. I can't tell you all about them because I can't remember now, but I know they're awfully nice in parts. A nice sort of place, and lovely people, and . . . and . . . '

'What about the going-away part?' She clenched her fists below the table because she had said such a dangerous, provocative thing.

Janet looked down into her empty mug

and swung it round as though swilling milk about at the bottom. 'Going away? Mm . . . I think that's what comes at the end. It's not the dreams I mind. It's when I'm leaving the place and . . . ' She looked quickly at her mother, surprised and unsure of herself; and then looked away.

Leaving the place, thought Mrs. Neal. And waking up. Was it leaving the land of her dream and being forced to wake up, or being unable to stay asleep any longer, that made Janet cry out in protest?

Her mouth was dry with fright. 'But where do I come in?' she persisted. 'It's me that you're afraid of leaving, isn't it? It's me that you call out to in your dream.'

'Do I?' Janet looked unnaturally cunning, quite unlike her usual self. 'I don't know. At least . . . I seem to remember being pulled away from my Mummy. But . . . ' She stopped. There was something in her mind which she would not let herself say. Abruptly she asked: 'Mummy, how do you know which is which?'

'How do you mean, dear?'

'Which is dreams and which is . . . the real thing?' Then her features puckered up and she began to cry.

Full of remorse, Mrs. Neal got up and went to put her arms round her daughter. She was surprised at the quiet resistance Janet offered.

They walked together to the village in an inexplicably hostile silence. The threatening grey sky weighed down heavily upon them.

* * *

Dr. Scott shook his head.

'I don't claim to be a witch doctor. There are times when I like some assistance in making my diagnosis. What am I supposed to be looking for, Mary? I can't find anything wrong.'

Mrs. Neal glanced at Janet.

The doctor said: 'Just sit in the room with the magazines, will you, Janet? We won't keep you waiting long.'

When the two of them were alone together he waited for Mrs. Neal to speak. It took her a few fumbling moments to get anything out. 'I don't know what to say. I mean — oh dear, Philip, I've forced myself to come here and get it all off my chest, and now I'm sure it'll sound a lot of nonsense.'

'Most of my patients trot out the most marvellous varieties of nonsense without feeling the slightest shame. Just reel off the symptoms and I'll trot out my answers.'

Symptoms? She told him as best she could, stumbling over this explanation of the inexplicable. When she had finished she wished she could have retracted every word. Overwhelmingly conscious that it was now broad daylight, she began to stammer out excuses and qualifications.

Dr. Scott shook his head brusquely. 'Don't try to back out now, Mary. You believed in what you were saying while you were saying it. There must be a reason for that. And if you think, now you've listened to your own story, that it sounds silly, there must be a reason for that, too. You're afraid, aren't you?'

'For Janet.'

'Are you sure of that? You feel that this

is something more than a physical matter — something more than just a tummy-ache. But is it really Janet who's suffering? Is Janet the patient, or . . . ?'

'I don't follow.'

'Let's be honest about it. You can be frank with me, Mary. Even more important, I want you to be frank with yourself. Are you sure' — he was speaking with great deliberation — 'that this nightmare, if it *is* a nightmare so far as Janet's concerned, is in itself worrying you? Are you sure it's not a little something in your subconscious which has been stirred up, so that you're reading things into the dream that aren't there?'

'I don't follow,' she said again.

'Perhaps you're too conscientious. You're too keyed-up about every little detail. I know what a struggle you've had and how lonely you've been.'

'Not lonely,' she said quickly; 'not with Janet there.'

'Aren't you perhaps asking too much of Janet? She's everything to you. I've no doubt you reproach yourself for every little thing that goes wrong with her, however insignificant. And when she dreams, you feel that her dreams show some sort of psychological dissatisfaction *with you*.'

'No. No, I don't think so. I don't look at things in that way. At least, I don't think I do.'

'You're too serious, Mary. You take things too earnestly.' She felt hopelessly that it was no good stopping him, no good telling him that he was on the wrong track altogether. 'In the first place,' he said brightly, 'is Janet frightened by these dreams?'

'She calls out for me as she's waking up.'

'But the dreams themselves — does she remember them in detail? Does she say they're horrible?'

'No,' Mrs Neal reluctantly admitted. 'She . . . she says they're quite nice.'

His gentle look of triumph was intolerable. So was his equally gentle offer to arrange for her to see a nerve specialist if she wished. And in the meantime, a tonic. Perhaps something soothing that would stop her worrying, until she herself came to accept that everything was all right.

She left him in a mood of rejection, as though she had been deserted by the only friend on whom she had relied. Janet walked silently beside her as they left the village and went back up the hill towards the forlorn little cottage, its bedroom windows like eyes watching them as they approached.

The doctor's voice rang in her head. Subconscious guilt about something — something absurd, as he had cheerfully assured her. You haven't neglected the child. You worry too much. The loss of her father wasn't your fault; you've done your best to fill his place; there's nothing with which to reproach yourself. Symbolism . . . child losing mother . . . insufficiency, guilt, pessimism . . . it's all in *your* mind, not in hers.

Just a recurrent dream — unusual, but nothing more.

And when, right at the end, suddenly bursting out with her fear, she had said, 'Do you believe in possession — in being possessed by . . . other forces?' he had risen from his chair and spoken to her gravely, an old friend concerned for her welfare, talking once more about nerve specialists and tonics and sedatives.

It was useless. How could she hope to convince him that it was not a prescription for a bottle of coloured liquid that she needed? While she repeated to herself the terrifying word 'possession' he talked about slight mental disturbances, strange fantasies. Unpleasant ideas, to be sure; but she would have been almost glad to believe him. When darkness crept down the hill and up from the village, encompassing the house, she would not have been frightened if only she could have attached a neat little clinical label to it all. A matter of psychology: it was a concept to drive out night fears, a comforting explanation of anything that made you uneasy. You could use it as a sort of magic charm, brandishing it in the face of monsters, spirits, phantoms. Anything would crumple and scuttle away before that cold, beautiful word.

If you believed in it.

* * *

When the first cry came that night, she sat down and picked up the book she had been reading, concentrating on the page at which it had lain open for a good fifteen minutes. No need to go upstairs. Janet was dreaming, but dreams could do no harm. It was better to stay downstairs. She herself was the only one who could suffer from hearing what went on in Janet's dreams. Symbolism, subconscious . . . she thought over the lovely musical syllables and tried to assure herself that they made everything all right.

She remained seated for a full ten minutes, and then put the book down because the print was tilting at absurd angles across the page and the sentences did not make sense and the lamplight did not seem as bright as it had been. She turned up the wick and carried the lamp upstairs.

Janet's quiet plaintive voice increased in volume as the door opened, like a radio sharply turned up.

'And down there by the pool . . . Mummy,

are we really together now? I'm sorry about last night, but I didn't know. Truly I didn't. I thought that was real. If it goes and happens again . . . but you won't let it, will you? You won't? But if it *did* happen again, I'd hold on tight like you said, and I'd still be me instead of being . . . whatever it was.'

Mrs. Neal lowered herself warily onto the edge of the bed. Janet uneasily turned her closed eyes towards the light.

'It's coming,' she moaned.

'I'm here, Jan. Wake up.' She wanted to seize Janet by the shoulders and shake her into wakefulness, but was afraid. She was scared to do more than speak slowly and clearly, hoping her voice would penetrate to that country beyond sleep where Janet was pausing indecisively.

'I'm here, Jan. You're all right. You're at home; you're safe. I'm not going away.'

'Mummy, it's come again. Hold me. I promise not to let go this time. And you won't let me, will you?'

'You're safe. No one's going to take you away.'

Janet twisted and burrowed into the

pillow as though to prevent herself waking up. The things she muttered were lost, but there was no mistaking the note of urgency. Mrs. Neal began to sob. She longed even more to reach out and shake her little girl. Surely it would be best done now, before it was too late? But she went on talking, not altogether sure of what she was saying. 'Janet, wake up, darling. Come along, now — I won't let you slip away.'

'It's coming,' said Janet tensely. 'But this time it'll be all right. I know it'll be all right. You promise, don't you? Promise. I'm me, and I'm staying me. I'll be back soon. Back right away.' She turned again, her eyelids fluttering as she screwed them up against the light.

'Jan . . . '

Janet's eyes opened. There was the same film that had been there before, then it slipped away, Janet was awake.

Mrs. Neal was trembling with the effort of expending all her forces in that mental strain, reaching into the unknown for her daughter. She let out a sigh now, and waited for the familiar smile. It was over.

Janet was back and now she would smile.

But there was no smile. No recognition. The hard, childishly honest eyes stared at her and the mouth twitched slightly. Janet said: 'Who are you?'

'Janet, wake up. The dream's all over and you're home. In bed. It's all over, darling.'

'Who are you?' repeated the child, drawing back.

Mrs. Neal gulped down the terror rising in her throat. She said desperately: 'You're home, Janet. Jan, don't look at me like that. You're all right now.'

'No. I'm lost now.' The girl let out a sudden cry of anguish. 'I'm lost. But I'm still me. I must remember that. This is the nightmare my Mummy told me about. This is it. But it'll be all right.'

'Janet, darling — '

'This is a nightmare,' said the child as though repeating a lesson. 'Soon I'll wake up again. Mummy said I would.'

Mrs. Neal reached out. But it was too late now. She knew it was too late. The little girl's eyes were wide open and she was cowering away, shaking her head in fear. ‘Leave me alone. Don’t touch me.’ The lamp threw great shadows under her eyes. ‘Who are you?’ She looked wildly about the room and recognised nothing. ‘When will I wake up?’ she cried. ‘Oh, when will I wake up?’

THE LOITERERS

He was so cold that soon he would be unable to put one foot in front of the other. It would be so much simpler to sink to the pavement, set his back against a wall, and let himself freeze to death. All that kept him going was the thought of the square, the flat, and Elizabeth.

It couldn't possibly be so cold — not in London, not even in February. There had been three bad weeks and a succession of power cuts; cisterns had frozen; but even the most pessimistic weather forecast hadn't warned of this all-pervading chill.

He crossed the main road. Something must be wrong with his eyes. The lights of buses and shop windows and restaurant doorways still shone, but all dimmed, all diffused through an icy haze.

At last he reached the shadow of the square. In the daytime, cars slotted in beside the parking meters. A couple of elderly women with silver-blue hair would walk their dachshunds parallel to the railings of the central garden: dogs were not allowed on the paths or grass within. The pub tucked away behind one corner did a brisk business with its cold lunch counter. At night the lights came on in an untidy jigsaw of windows. The square went quiet then, though it was never entirely deserted: perhaps because of the secretive shade of the trees overhanging the railings, there were occasional bursts of activity — dark shapes drifting in from the nearby brightness, and a sighing which might have been whispers of love or subdued laughter.

Now, as he crossed towards that unforgettable door, there were surely more people around than usual. Not quite as shadowy as usual, but as real and solid as himself.

A man brushed past him.

There was something familiar about the set of those shoulders. Bernard hurried to keep up. There was agony in his legs and arms and head. He tried to call out. The man looked uncertainly over his shoulder and flapped one hand as though brushing away a cobweb. As he went into the cramped entrance hall of the block of flats, light by the stairwell sharpened his profile.

It couldn't be. Mustn't be.

He had to be stopped. Had to be dragged back before he got to Elizabeth. For his own sake . . . or Elizabeth's?

* * *

They had met late in December, in that sluggish drag of days between Christmas and New Year. He hadn't meant to go out that evening. Coming in from the under-staffed, apathetic office he had showered, changed, and poured himself a large whisky. Then he picked up the *Radio Times* and tried to find a television programme banal but competent enough to lull him into a cosy trance.

The telephone was only a few inches from his right hand. He wasn't going to ring anyone. It was too feeble, the results too predictable. Chop suey or saltimbocca with some girl who bored him. Or a drink with poor old Chris, or with Neil and Marion — no, definitely not Neil and Marion: at this time of year they would be especially boozed-up and quarrelsome.

The flat was so empty. For two years Susan had been here, expecting him to marry her; and he'd sort of half meant to; but after two years the credibility gap had stretched a bit wide, and just before Christmas she'd gone.

By half past seven he was straining towards the phone, fidgeting to become involved in something . . . anything.

It breathed its tinkling pre-echo and began to ring.

It was Neil. 'Bernard? Caught you in. Great. What about dropping in for a bite to eat?'

'Well, I . . . when would this be?'

'Right now. Make up a foursome.' Neil sounded slurred, but was pungent enough when Marion called out something from a distance and he yelled back: 'Aw, belt up. I'm *asking* him, aren't I?'

No, not Neil and Marion. Not tonight. 'It's very nice of you, Neil,' he said, 'but I really do have a lot to do at the moment.'

'Like opening a tin of baked beans?'

'I've got a lot of scraps to get rid of, in fact.'

'Us too. That's why we're inviting you. Get cracking, or I'll bloody well come and fetch you.'

Always with Neil there was the possibility that he might do something just like that. The jolly bluster could turn sour. It was always easier, and a lot less noisy, to go along with him.

Bernard drove resentfully along the familiar route, swearing that this time he would leave early. The later it got, the more Neil and Marion quarrelled with each other. The only way to deflect them was to announce that you really must go, and then they'd unite against you and curse in concert at the tops of their voices.

'Come on, come on, for crying out loud.' Neil flung open the door. 'Where the hell have you been?'

Marion's long, meaty legs sprawled from a chair on the far side of the sitting-room. 'Bernie, love. Hello. Gorgeous of you to come. Neil, don't stand there like a spare candle at a wake.

Introduce him to Elizabeth.'

'She's *your* friend,' said Neil boisterously, 'Why — '

'I can't get up. I've been slaving over a hot risotto all day.'

'That'll make a change from dried-up turkey, anyway.'

'Oh, give it a rest.'

The young woman looked fragile beside the other two. Marion, tall and handsome, with bright complexion and large rigid mouth, was a good match for her massive husband. Elizabeth was as alien as a Persian cat between two unkempt Airedales. Her hair was fine pale russet, her eyes a smoky green.

Her hand was cool and unresponsive in Bernard's.

'Doesn't seem possible.' Marion jerked one thumb at Neil to indicate that she wanted her glass refilled. 'All these years we've known Elizabeth, and all the time we've known you, Bernie, and somehow you two've never met.'

Having been introduced, Elizabeth appeared to lose interest, if she had ever felt any in the first place. She withdrew into herself, her head back against her chair, resting smooth arms along the brown and gold fabric.

Neil sloshed whisky into a tumbler and handed it to Bernard. 'Glad you could make it. Down with drink.'

Marion pushed herself up with a groan. 'Well, I suppose I'd better think about dishing up.'

'I'll come with you.' Elizabeth's muted voice had a throb of latent, unreleased music. 'I'll give you a hand.'

'No, you stay and talk.'

Elizabeth did not argue. She simply went out with Marion towards the kitchen.

Neil said: 'Nice bit of how's-your-father, eh?'

'Haven't had much chance to size her up, so far.'

'And you won't get much chance. Wouldn't waste my time, if I were you.'

'Funny we haven't met before.'

'She doesn't come here all that often. Just that Marion gets it into her head every now and then to ring her, and go on ringing until she gets her way. You know how Marion is.' Bernard restrained a laugh. Neil swilled whisky round his glass and peered into it. 'Wait till they get going,' he said. 'All that jolly old school chum business. Remember the famous occasion when Lucy Locket lost her biology specimen down the loo? It's always famous, everything's a *famous* occasion, especially if nobody's ever heard of it. Bunfights in the dorm from now till doomsday. Marion,' he said vindictively, 'is the worst.'

It was true that Marion did most of the talking over dinner, and true that she talked mainly about schooldays. Their school was the only possible connection between two women so utterly different. Elizabeth contributed only a few offhand remarks.

Bernard was conscious that she was avoiding his gaze. It was not that she was shy: she was above and beyond shyness. They had been introduced; they were sitting at the same table; she would see the evening through to its end, and that was that.

He couldn't take his eyes off her.

The pattern of the evening was just as he had foreseen. When he tried to refuse more large libations of whisky after dinner, Neil grew belligerent. Elizabeth, with no more than a tremor of the head, somehow ducked beneath Neil's wrath. Neil turned on Marion. The theme of the row was unidentifiable: after ten years they didn't need a formal excuse for a squabble.

Elizabeth said: 'I really must go.'

'No,' said Neil sharply.

'Me, too.' Bernard seized the opportunity to get up, trying to catch Elizabeth's eye and offer a quick smile of collusion.

'Sit down,' growled Neil. 'Here, give me your glass — and sit *down*.'

Bernard said to Elizabeth: 'I'll give you a lift.'

'Oh, no. Please. It's quite all right.'

He couldn't believe her flutter of immediate panic was real. She must have caught Neil's and Marion's tendency to exaggerate, to blow up every word and gesture.

'I'll ring for a taxi for you,' said Neil unexpectedly.

At last she smiled. It was fleeting, elusive, and made Bernard want to go on and on looking at her until it came again.

She said: ‘Yes, I’ll have a taxi, thank you.’

‘Not the way it’s pelting down out there, you won’t,’ said Marion.

They had been unaware of the drumming on the window panes until now. When Bernard looked out, the rain was a shimmering turbulence across the road.

Elizabeth had to accept Bernard’s offer. When he asked for her address she hesitated, as though even at this late stage hoping to find a way of not committing herself. Then she sighed, and said: ‘Withersedge Square.’

He drove down into Chelsea, glancing every now and then at the tilt of her head. Street lights flicked gold sparks from her hair. She stared straight ahead through the swishing arc of the windscreen wiper. When he was slowing across King’s Road and up one side of the square, he said: ‘What number?’

‘Oh, just put me down here. This’ll do nicely.’

'Right to your door,' he insisted. 'I'm not going to dump you out in that.'

Her head dropped a fraction. 'Twenty-three.'

He slowed to a crawl and saw the figures on a transom over an open door. Within was the glint of lift gates.

'It's very kind of you. Good night.' She was out and on the second of three steps up to the door before he could hurry round the car.

He said: 'Are you doing anything New Year's Eve?'

'I'm afraid so, yes.' She was not waiting for the lift, but starting up the stairs.

'Perhaps I could ring you sometime.'

'It was sweet of you' — an eerie, quivering strand of music down the resonant stairwell — 'to drive me home.'

He drove back to his empty flat. Not very rewarding company, Elizabeth. Her mysterious silence was probably not mysterious at all: simply that she had nothing to say.

Yet he lay awake and thought about her eyes and about the glowing silken threads of her hair.

By the middle of the following afternoon he had persuaded himself that it was only polite to ring his hostess with thanks for the evening.

Marion sounded surly and surprised. 'Getting formal in our old age, aren't we?' There was a sound which could have been a yawn. Probably the skirmish with Neil had been protracted long after their guests had left.

'Pleasant girl, your friend.

'Pleasant?' There was a pause. 'That's the last word I'd use for her.'

'I thought you were old friends.'

'Oh, we are, lovey, we are. I just meant . . . oh, it's so hard to say what you do mean when you're talking about Elizabeth. I've known her since we were at school and still I don't know a teeny-weeny thing about her. Tell you one thing — she hates anyone calling her Liz. Something significant in that, I've always thought.'

'You make her sound fascinating.'

'Oh,' said Marion. 'Oh. It's like that, is it?'

'I was only saying — '

'Yes, I heard you. You won't get anywhere, Bernie.'

He could hardly bear to risk it: 'She's got somebody else?'

'There's always been a fair assortment of dewy-eyed creeps. But they've never lasted — just drifted off, never been seen again.'

'So nobody permanent.'

'I've never been sure about that. I mean, I've had a hunch there's been some long-term thing in the background — one of those interminable, dismal things with some married man who's always going to leave his wife but never does. You know.'

'No,' said Bernard, 'I don't know.' And he wasn't going to let himself think any such thing.

'If I were you' — Marion was suddenly sharp and hostile — 'I wouldn't start from here.'

She hung up.

* * *

He paced round Withersedge Square two evenings in succession. He needed a walk, and it was silly to stick so slavishly to his own immediate neighbourhood. Once he went into the pub and ordered a half of draught lager, but as soon as it was poured he hastened to knock it back in case something had happened in the square while he was inside.

There were other loiterers — some huddled against the railings of the garden pressed together, murmuring, while others seemed as aimless as himself. On one occasion he saw a shadow move up the steps of the flats, and wanted to run round the square, to follow, to see if this was a visitor for Elizabeth.

Of course there had to be *somebody*. With a woman as lovely as Elizabeth, there must be someone. Someone who had made her sad, remote; someone who could never hope to give her happiness.

The shadow could have been the tenant of one of the other flats. There must be fifteen or sixteen of them in the block.

The next night he forced himself to stay indoors and play records.

Sunday lunchtime he again walked

down to Chelsea. It was a cold, bright day. He might meet someone he knew in one of the pubs, have a drink, talk, find somewhere to eat. There was no hurry. It was that sort of Chelsea Sunday — languid, for all its icy gutters.

Elizabeth came out of a side-street delicatessen. He savoured her as she approached — her head pensively lowered, her right arm swinging the string bag to and fro, her shoulders moving in a drowsy rhythm beneath a light curry-yellow shirt too flimsy for this winter morning.

He said: 'Good morning. If you're hungry, I promise to offer something better than your packet of pizza.'

Her eyes were downright insulting in the way they unguardedly said: Oh, no — not *you*.

He talked fast and flippantly; desperately. She shook her head. He put his hand possessively under her elbow, and through the fabric of the shirt felt that it was ice-cold. There was a newly fashionable bistro a few yards away. Perhaps because of the cold and because of the warm smell seeping out, or because she thought it's the middle of the day, it's a nothing, it doesn't have to lead to anything, she let herself be steered inside.

As though to mock him, she ordered *pizza*.

He said it had been a nice evening with Neil and Marion, and she said yes, hadn't it. He asked if she'd been in here before, and she said yes, a couple of times.

He said: 'I believe the Congreve at the Aldwych is pretty good.'

'Is it? I hadn't heard.'

'You like musicals . . . or opera?'

'I don't think so,' she said distantly.

It was bright and harsh outside, but there were wooden slats across the windows and candles flickered above Chianti bottles on the tables. Bernard leaned towards her. The yellow flame fluttered in his breath.

'It strikes me,' he said, 'there's a lot you have to learn about yourself.'

'Me?' she said. 'Or you?'

'We could make it a joint effort.'

At last she looked steadily, deliberately

at him. She said: 'It's no good, you know. It really isn't.'

'There's somebody else?'

She could have asked him what that had to do with him, or simply not answered at all. Instead, after a fraction of second, she said: 'Yes, that's it. I'm afraid so.'

It was too quick. She might have been grasping it as the easiest way of getting rid of him. He wondered if she, too, had telephoned Marion to thank her; or if Marion had been the one to do the telephoning; and how they might have talked, all girls together.

And then a little subsiding trickle of words was forced out of her, as though some painful inner honesty wouldn't let her leave it as unequivocal as that. 'I don't see him all the time,' she said. 'But that's how it is. I mean, nothing else is any good. I'm sorry.'

When they left the restaurant he fell into step beside her. She stopped and held out her hand.

'I'll see you to your door,' he said.

'No, really.'

'You're always saying no to things. One fine day you'll have to try saying yes.'

'It's saying yes that leads to . . . to all the misery.' Her gold-swathed head shone as she walked off. Bernard hurried to catch up with her. Sunlight bronzed a crease in her shirt where it dipped over the swell of her breast.

'I dare you.' He was beside her as she turned the corner into the square. 'Try someone else for a change. Just as an antidote. Disillusionment's not a drug you can live on for ever.'

She stopped at the foot of the three steps. 'What do you know about illusion, or disillusion — *really* know?'

'If one really knew, there'd be no illusions.'

'Oh, dear. What are we talking about?'

'About you coming to the theatre with me. And to dinner. And playing it by ear from then on.' A shadow flitted across the corner of his eye. He had a momentary sensation of being watched. But when he glanced sharply to one side, there was nobody there.

Only Elizabeth was still watching him.

He had dared her. For some reason she had to pick up the challenge — and yet offer him one more chance to retreat. She said: 'You're quite sure?'

'I'm very persistent.'

'Yes.' Her sigh was one of ultimate resignation. 'All right.' It was a warning as much as a promise. 'But it would have been better not. Much better.'

He took her to the Aldwych, to the ballet, to a concert, to dinner. At her door — always at her door, not a step further — he kissed her. Her lips were always cool. Even when, after a spicy dinner and several fiery apricot brandies in a Hungarian restaurant, he caught her shoulder as they emerged into the street and spun her close to him and kissed her, he found no warmth and no taint on her steady, cold breath.

Neil bumped into him in the City one lunchtime and bawled: 'What's all this we hear about you and Liz?'

He remembered Marion saying that Elizabeth hated being called Liz. Rightly so. It didn't fit — least of all coming from Neil's heavy, wet lips.

'I didn't know there was anything to hear.'

'Look, this is your old mate, remember? Come and have a quick one, and we'll swap a few juicy secrets.'

Bernard refused, loathing the mere idea of Elizabeth's name being mentioned between them.

Later he wondered what they had heard and who had told them. Elizabeth chattering to Marion? Again, it didn't fit.

On a steel-grey Sunday they drove out into Essex, had lunch, and drove around and came back after dark. Now she no longer stared rigidly ahead, but glanced repeatedly at him as though to assess if he was the right one. Occasionally she leaned towards him and tentatively brushed her cheek against his shoulder. He heard her faintly, meditatively singing to herself.

When they reached the block of flats she stopped on the bottom step and looked beyond him into the agitated flurry of shadows along the railings. Bernard felt that someone was plucking at his sleeve.

He was abruptly sure that for her it had been a farewell day. She was going to say sorry and all that, but she didn't want to see him anymore. The other man was coming back: perhaps was already back? The one she'd never be free of. A paralysing hatred twisted in his belly.

She said: 'Why not come and have dinner with *me* for a change? Here — Thursday evening?'

'I . . . can't think of anything nicer.'

They kissed. Was she a little more responsive, leaving her lips against his just a little longer?

As he walked jubilantly away he could have sworn she cried, 'I'm sorry, oh I'm so sorry.' It must be his own delayed reaction: he had been so positive she was about to say sorry, she didn't want him to bother her any more, that the words had gone on ringing in his head.

On the Thursday he was as surprised to find her flat was four-square and ordinary as he had been to learn that she had an ordinary name and an ordinary telephone number. She had a few pieces of jade, a Staffordshire porcelain cottage, and a framed photograph of a lean-featured man who might have been her father: he was surely too old, and the yellowing picture itself too old, to be her intermittent, unsatisfying lover.

They started with honeydew melon and went on to a veal dish with a dozen conflicting flavours which he knew were delicious but on which he couldn't concentrate. Elizabeth had never been so gay — frenetically gay. She laughed, and looked into his eyes, and they talked across each other and laughed, and her head went back and she glowed. She was wearing a white sleeveless dress adorned only with a narrow strip of silver braid at the high neck and round her waist, like two circlets of finely crushed ice. After the meal she brought coffee to the couch and sat beside him.

When she turned towards him there was a flash of stark terror in the sea-swelling green of her eyes . . . then a fatalistic demand which had to be appeased.

A standard lamp shone brightly behind his shoulder. He twisted round, reaching for the switch.

'No,' said Elizabeth.

After her early indifference and silence and evasions he would have expected that when at last she surrendered there would have to be, at most, the discreet twilight of a shaded lamp. But she switched on an overhead light to add to the glare of the standard lamp and, standing in the middle of the room, pulled her dress over her head. She was wearing nothing underneath. In the stark light she came white out of the white sheath.

He reached for her.

'It'll be all right,' she said fiercely, close to his ear, to herself rather than to him. 'This time it's *got* to be.'

Then, as he bore her down upon the couch, it seemed that he immediately lost her. She fled into her old self. Her body accepted his but her mind was elsewhere: she was twisting her head from side to side, peering over his right shoulder and then his left.

At the same time she moved in his arms like subtle yet clamorous music. She moaned sweetly against his throat. And she burned like ice — for still she was unrelentingly cold wherever he touched her.

Against one wall he glimpsed a wispy thread drifting like a streamer of cigarette smoke.

Then he sank, spent, on her shoulder; his damp brow against her unchanged, un-warmed flesh.

The lights dipped, fluttered, and went out.

From the sudden sparking darkness the tormented faces rushed in on him. He knew some of them — must have half seen, in the square, the features which were now so plain. Elizabeth moaned again, seized again by terror. The faces contorted into a new pattern. They could see her every movement in spite of the sudden black-out. Lips drooped; their sigh was a pitiful dying breeze all about the room. They watched because they could not bear not to watch. Their faces, Bernard thought insanely, were like those of starving men pressed to a bakery window

'I'm sorry.' Elizabeth was struggling to

free herself. 'Bernard, I didn't want . . . I didn't *want* . . . '

He floundered away from her and barked his shin against a coffee table. It was grotesque. He tried to laugh. 'Hell of a time for a power cut.' Groping for the end of the couch, he managed to steady himself.

The lights came on again.

'Please go.' She was huddling in on herself,

'Elizabeth. Darling Elizabeth — '

'Please.' It was a cry of hopelessness beyond telling. 'I should never have . . . *please* go.'

He shivered. He was still shivering as he went downstairs, accompanied by wraiths looping in jealous despair around him, bobbing like midges as he crossed the square and stumbled towards home.

A knot of ice swelled in his chest. Spiky tentacles reached out through his veins and scraped his lungs. In bed, the blankets didn't warm him. Cold clawed up into them from his body and defeated them.

A picture of Elizabeth shaped itself in

the air above him, her face wrenched by anguish or ecstasy.

He thought of that other man who had been around for so long, who might come back. Elizabeth had never promised he wouldn't come back.

He sat up and snapped on the light. She receded, as the haunting faces had receded when the lights went on again in her flat.

An interminable time passed. But if it was interminable, how could it pass? All an illusion. He got up, because he had to see Elizabeth. Without any consciousness of having dressed, he found himself in the night streets. Only they weren't streets, but vast chasms. He lost his way. The only reality was the throbbing agony of every step he took.

Until at last here he was, again, in the square. And the man he recognised was going upstairs, and they were grasping with gossamer fingers at him.

'Neil, don't! You don't *know* . . . '

Neil, unhearing, reached the second floor. At Elizabeth's door he took out a key and let himself in.

* * *

They were sucked up the stairwell and into the room after him.

Bernard fought the nightmare, hammering his face and chest with his fists, telling himself to wake up, slamming his hands together. There was no sensation other than that of ultimate deprivation. How could there be so much pain when his entire body was so numb?

Over Neil's shoulder they all yearned into Elizabeth's implacably radiant face. She knew they were there, but had eyes only for Neil.

'Missed me, Liz? Nothing like keeping 'em eager, that's what I always say.'

Bernard refused to let himself believe in anything as crude and impossible and obscene as this. He clawed at Neil's shoulder. His attendant shades rustled their sad laughter. There were so many of them — so real and substantial now.

He realised, with a horror still not clear, that somehow he had become one with them.

'And what about our friend Bernard,

then?' Neil was taking off his jacket and tie. He began to unbutton his shirt. 'You've heard about poor old Bernie?'

'I read about it.' The admission was flat and unemotional. 'I was sorry. It was . . . tragic.'

'Something fishy, y'know. All the symptoms of freezing to death, and there he was in a flat seething with central heating. I've heard of giving people the cold shoulder, but honestly' — he bellowed a laugh — 'what *did* you do to him, gorgeous? What did you do, Liz?'

She hates anyone calling her Liz . . .

Yes. Her dilated eyes were awash with loathing as Neil took her. Loathing and uncontrollable longing.

Bernard ached to flee downstairs and out into the nowhere of the square. But he had to watch. He was one of the damned now, and it was their fate to watch as Elizabeth gave herself up to loud-mouthed Neil with his brutish hands and rutting self-confidence.

Not until it was ended and Neil had had a drink and kissed Elizabeth offhandedly and promised offhandedly that he'd come back when he could manage it, was there any escape. Then, as Neil whistled jauntily down the stairs, they sighed after him and watched him go and dispersed around the square to dance their eternal ephemeral dance.

Neil wouldn't be stricken as they had been stricken. Neil was immune. Neil — an absurd echo from a world Bernard no longer belonged to — didn't feel the cold.

Other men would venture up those stairs to Elizabeth's door. And she would say no and then be coaxed into saying her despairing yes. And the prisoners of the square would be doomed to follow and watch and yearn and weep their impotent tears.

Was there to be no respite from lust and jealousy throughout all eternity?

The shadows brooded by the railings and did sentry-duty in front of the block of flats, a few yards from the traffic and the lights and the living flesh, but a world away. Here were only shadows and insubstantial railings, and bare trees within the garden.

And no bird sang.

PARTY GAMES

The moment Alice Jarman opened the front door and saw Simon Potter on the step, she knew that there would be trouble.

Behind her the party was growing noisy. Already a fight had broken out. Two boys were shouting at each other and there was an occasional thump as one or other of them was thrown heavily against the wall. But it was the usual sort of fight. A party at which small boys didn't fight wasn't much of a party.

Simon Potter said: 'Good afternoon, Mrs Jarman.'

He was eight years of age and he was not the kind of boy who would become involved in a fight. He was polite, neat, quiet, and clever and he was unpopular. His unpopularity was such as to keep him out of a scuffle rather than bring one down upon him. He was a cold little boy. Even as he stood there with his deferential smile he gave Alice the shivers.

He wore a new raincoat, his shoes were highly polished — probably by himself, she thought — and his pallid brown hair was sleeked back. He carried a neatly wrapped present.

Alice stepped back. Simon came on into the hall. At the same moment the door of the sitting-room was flung back and Ronnie came pounding out. He stopped when he saw Simon. He said what Alice had been sure he would say.

'I didn't invite *him*.'

'Now, Ronnie — '

'Many happy returns, Ronnie,' said Simon, holding out the package.

Ronnie could not help looking at it. He could not help the instinctive movement of his hand towards it. Then he shook his head and looked up at Alice.

'But, Mum . . . '

She smoothed it over — or, rather, blurred it over. The noise and exuberance from the sitting-room helped. Ronnie was unable to concentrate. He wanted to stay and argue, wanted to accept the present, and wanted to get back into the uproar.

The three things bubbled up and blended in his mind. Alice took Simon's coat and steered him towards the gaiety. He didn't need to be told to wipe his feet; he added nothing to the muddy treads which some of them had left. Ronnie tried to say something, but somehow he was holding the package, and then he began to unwrap it as he followed Simon into the room.

Alice stood by the door for a minute or two and looked in.

'Hey . . . look . . . super!' Ronnie tossed shreds of paper aside and opened the box within. He took out a model crane and held it up.

'It's battery-operated,' said Simon quietly.

It was a simple statement, but it wiped the pleasure off Ronnie's face. The others, who had crowded closer, edged back and turned to stare at Simon. His present was more expensive than any which they had brought. He had done the wrong thing. He was always doing the wrong thing. The fact that he did a thing made it wrong.

A large boy with carroty hair pushed Ronnie. Ronnie put the crane on a chair and pushed him back. A girl with a blue hair-ribbon said, 'Oh, don't start that again,' and stepped to one side. She found herself close to Simon. He smiled. He looked at her, and then at another girl a few feet away, as though to draw them both nearer to him. 'Always talking to girls,' Ronnie had once said of Simon to his mother. Alice watched. Yes, she could see that he was a boy who would talk to girls, because he had nothing to say to boys. But the girls were not flattered. Instead of listening to him they giggled and made eyes at each other and then scurried away, looking back and still giggling.

Alice went towards the kitchen and drew the curtains. It would soon be quite dark outside. In summer they could have had the party in the garden; but Ronnie had elected to be born in the winter, so most of his celebrations had been accompanied by a trampling of wet feet into the house and a great fussing over scarves and gloves and rain hoods and mackintoshes when the guests left.

Tom would be home in another twenty minutes or so. She would be glad to see him. Even though the din would not diminish, it would somehow be more tolerable when shared. Tom would organise games, jolly them all along, and make the little girls in particular shriek with laughter. Until he came she couldn't concentrate on the food or on anything else. She had to keep dashing back to the sitting-room to make sure that nobody was really getting hurt and nobody was being neglected. She had started them off on a game of musical chairs, but her piano playing was pretty terrible; and while she had been at the keyboard there had been chaos behind her, since she had suggested a treasure hunt, only to realise that she had done nothing about hiding the treasure before the party started.

She was not very good at organising parties. The sheer pressure of the children's excitement overpowered her. No matter how much trouble she took in the days beforehand, when the birthday itself came she was never ready for it. Not that it mattered, Tom assured her. Just open the door, let 'em in, and leave 'em to it. When there were signs of the furniture cracking up under the strain, bring on the sandwiches and jelly and cake and ice cream.

It was all very well for Tom. He did not get home until after she had taken the first shock of the impact. Twenty children together were not just twenty separate children added together, one plus one plus one and so on: they combined into something larger and more terrifying. There was no telling what they might do if the circumstances were right . . . or wrong, depending on the way you looked at it.

There was a howl of derision from the sitting-room. Alice nerved herself to go and make another inspection.

By the time she got there it was impossible to tell what the cause of the howl had been. Simon Potter was backed against a wall, while Ronnie and his best friend grinned and bobbed their heads with a lunatic merriment, exaggerating the movement, slapping their sides like bad actors in a school play.

Ronnie saw his mother watching him. His grin became genuine and affectionate. Then, before she could frown or ask him a silent question, he swung round and gathered up an armful of his presents.

'Come and look! Look what my dad gave me!'

Somebody groaned theatrically; a boy with pimples blew a loud raspberry. But they all gathered obediently round. It was the accepted thing to do. This was Ronnie's party and Ronnie's birthday, and at some stage it was only fair that he should insist on their inspecting his trophies.

'My dad gave me this.' Alice felt soft inside at the sound of adoration in his voice. 'And this. My dad gave me this as well.' It would have been just the same if Tom had given him a cheap scribbling pad or a box of crayons: the devotion would have been there, unwavering. She loved him for loving so intensely.

Simon was watching gravely. He showed neither excitement nor boredom.

He did not make approving noises, and he did not exchange glances of sly boredom with anyone. He was remote, dispassionate, unmoved.

Yet somewhere behind that bleak little face there must be envy or, at the very least, sadness. Simon's father had died years ago. His mother had brought him up with a single-minded fervour that allowed him no relaxation and little contact with other children, even though he spent so many hours and days and weeks at school with them. She worked hard in a solicitor's office and managed to run the home as well, determined that the boy should not feel the loss of his father too deeply. Each afternoon he stayed on at school for an hour in a class set aside for children with difficult journeys, difficult home backgrounds, or with working parents who could not leave their jobs in time to meet their children. By the time he did get home Mrs Potter was in the house waiting for him, ready to devote herself to him. She was proud of the life they made together, proud of their home, and proud of Simon's unfailing neatness and politeness and cleverness.

Alice saw him clear his throat. She saw it rather than heard it — the way he ducked his chin and gulped. He edged forward. She thought for a moment that he was going to ask if he could have a closer look at one of Ronnie's presents. Then he said: 'What about a game?'

The heads turned. They stared at him. It was a little girl who broke the sudden silence. She seemed glad of the diversion. 'Yes. Let's do something. What shall we play?'

'If we could get some pieces of paper' — Simon glanced swiftly at Alice and she realised that all along he must have been aware of her scrutiny — 'we could put someone's name on it and — '

'Oh, *paper* games,' groaned someone.

'Choose a name,' Simon persisted, 'and write it down one side of the paper. Then divide the paper up into squares, and have, say, flowers and trees and the names of — well, footballers if you like — and they have to begin with the letters of the name.'

The boy who specialised in blowing

raspberries blew another. 'What's he talking about?' said the girl with the blue hair-ribbon.

'It's easy.' Simon's voice rose pleadingly. 'You write the name down one side of the paper. Then you write the things you're going to have across the top — that is, I mean, the categories you've chosen. And — '

'Oh, *paper* games.'

Alice intervened. It was time for an adult to take control and tell them what to do. She walked into the room and tried desperately to recall the games they had played when she was a child. Her mind refused to render up its memories. All she could remember was a girl going through the seat of a chair and screaming, and a squat little boy who had gathered an audience around him while he practised spitting into the fire. She said: 'Now, everybody.' They turned thankfully towards her. 'What about Postman's Knock?' she ventured.

There were shrugs and hisses and moans; but the girls squealed hopefully and nudged one another, and in no time at all they were playing Postman's Knock. Alice retreated again, leaving them to it. From the kitchen door she glanced occasionally across the hall and then felt absurdly like a voyeur. Some of the boys behaved with a flamboyant confidence that indicated a prolonged study of films which they ought never to have been allowed to see. Some of the girls wriggled; others relaxed and enjoyed themselves. It was frightening to see in these children of eight and nine years of age the pattern of what they would be as adults — patterns already forming, some already established.

And there was Simon outside the door, waiting. He knocked. The girl who came looked at him warily, prepared to be haughty or coquettish. After they had kissed she wiped her lips with the back of her hand. Simon went back into the room. The girl looked up at the ceiling and said, loudly enough for him and the others inside to hear: 'Ugh!'

They soon tired — the boys sooner than the girls.

'Murder. Let's play murder!'

As the door opened and Ronnie came racing out, Alice tried to assemble good reasons why they should not play murder. She was not quick enough. Already they were racing upstairs. Two boys came into the kitchen, making for the back door, and stopped when they saw her.

'Not outside,' said Alice quickly. This, at any rate, she could prevent. 'It's too muddy in the back garden. You've got to stay indoors.'

They turned and dashed away. She heard footsteps pounding overhead. There was a distant slamming of doors. Lights were switched off. Ronnie appeared suddenly in the splash of brightness thrown out from the kitchen. He and the pimply boy were grinning and whispering. Simon Potter passed them on his way towards the stairs. As he went they clutched each other conspiratorially.

Before Alice could make a move, Ronnie swung towards her. 'Don't mind if we close the door, Mum?' He did not wait for an answer, but closed it quietly and made her a prisoner. She knew there would be yells of protest if she opened it again.

There was a full minute of uneasy silence. In her head it was incongruously noisier than the last hour had been. In the hush a tension was building up. Something was going to snap.

A muffled thump came from upstairs. It was repeated. It might have been somebody banging insistently on the floor or somebody hammering to be let out. If, she thought apprehensively, they had locked somebody into one of the rooms or one of the old cupboards at the far end of the landing . . . the creaky, cold end of this old, cold house . . . Somebody. Simon.

Then there was a convincingly bloodcurdling scream.

Alice jerked the door open. 'Put that light out!'

'No, it's all right' — Ronnie's voice came from the landing — 'it's over.'

Feet pounded downstairs again. Lights were snapped on everywhere. Everyone was shouting at everyone else. Who had been murdered? Who was it?

To Alice's relief the victim was Marion

Pickering, a fluffy little blonde with eyes too knowing for her years. There was indeed quite a possibility, thought Alice uncharitably, that Marion would finish up on the front page of certain Sunday newspapers.

Boys and girls swarmed out of every cranny. The hall seemed to boil with activity, then they were all jostling into the sitting-room. There seemed to be twice as many people here as when the party began.

She could hear the shouting. Ronnie was trying to establish some kind of order.

'Who was on the stairs . . . shut up, will you . . . we've got to find who was upstairs and who was downstairs. Now sit down . . . oh, shut up a minute, will you . . . '

The inquiry was going to be a disorderly one. It needed a strong hand to control it. Instead, there was a shouting and shrieking, a carry-over from the tenseness in the dark.

It was really dark now. Alice had not realised how swiftly the evening had taken over. Twenty minutes earlier it would still have been too hazy to play murder; now there was blackness outside the windows.

Through the hubbub of voices she heard a faint but unmistakable sound. It was Tom's key in the front door.

She was halfway across the hall as he came in. 'Darling!'

He had to lean precariously forward to kiss her. He was laden with an armful of garden tools — a trowel sticking out of some torn brown paper, a pair of secateurs, and a short-handled axe. 'Going well?' He nodded towards the sitting-room door.

'I'm so glad you're back.'

'Ah. That means it's getting out of hand, mm?'

'Any minute now.'

It was so wonderful to see him. His lean, furrowed face was so reassuring. The smell of pipe smoke in his hair, the quiet confidence in his eyes, the sight of his competent, capable hands: everything about him strengthened her and at the same time soothed her.

Yet there was something wrong. Something nagged at her and demanded her attention.

As he turned to lay the garden tools across the umbrella stand she realised that the sound was still going on upstairs — the intermittent thumping she had heard earlier.

'I'll just dump these,' Tom was saying, 'and then plunge into the fray.'

She was jolted into awareness of what he had done with the tools.

'Don't leave them there! For goodness' sake! With all these little monsters in and out . . . '

'All right, all right. I'll take them out to the shed right away.'

'It's filthy out there. You'll get mud all over your shoes if . . . ' She broke off and laughed, and Tom laughed. 'I do sound a nagger, don't I?' she said.

He tucked the implements under his arm and headed for the stairs. 'I'll leave them in our room,' he said firmly.

Ronnie emerged abruptly and ecstatically from the sitting-room. 'Dad!' He threw himself at his father and butted him, tried to get one arm round him, smiled up at him. ‘Come on in here — come and see — I’ve got lots more things. But nothing like you gave me.’

‘In a minute or two, son. I’ve just got to go upstairs with some things. I’ll be right down.’

Alice looked past them into the sitting-room. She moved closer to the door. Then she said: ‘Ronnie, where’s Simon?’

‘Mm?’

‘Simon. Where is he?’

Ronnie shrugged and pummelled his father again. ‘Dunno. Probably gone up to the lavatory.’

‘Ronnie, if you’ve done anything . . . locked him in anywhere . . . ’

‘Don’t be long, Dad.’ Ronnie twisted away and slid cunningly past his mother. She could not bring herself to pursue him into that whirlpool of arms and legs and boisterous faces.

Tom said: ‘Anything wrong?’

‘I don’t know. I just wonder if they’ve played some horrid joke on Simon Potter.’

'Didn't think he'd been invited.'

'He wasn't. But he came, poor kid. They've kept him on the edge of things. And now I think they've done something.' The din from the sitting-room was so overpowering that she could not swear to hearing the spasmodic thudding from above. 'If they've locked him in one of the cupboards, or one of the rooms at the far end of the landing . . . '

'I'll see,' said Tom reassuringly.

She was glad to turn away towards the kitchen and leave it all to him. Now everything was going to be all right.

Two boys scuttled out of the sitting-room. 'Mrs Jarman — where is it, please?'

'First door on the left at the top of the stairs.'

They went up two stairs at a time behind Tom. Alice felt comfortable and safe when she returned to the kitchen, instead of being a frightened outcast. She began to put the cups of jelly on a large tray. In another fifteen minutes they could start eating. After that, Tom would organise them while she cleared the food away and did the washing-up.

Ronnie came in. 'Mum, where's the stuff for the game? You know, the corpse stuff.'

The thudding upstairs had stopped. But there was a louder thump, as though someone had fallen or banged something heavy against the floor. Perhaps it was Tom wrenching open one of the cupboard doors: they were old, stiff, and misshapen.

'Ronnie,' she began, '*did you* — '

He did not wait for her to finish. He scooped up the small tray that he had so carefully prepared earlier today, covered with a sheet of thin brown paper, and was gone again.

She heard him yelling at the top of his voice. 'All right, everyone. Come on, sit down. Now, I'm going to put the lights out . . . '

'Hey, wait for us!' Footsteps hastened down the stairs and two or three boys dashed into the sitting-room. They must have been queueing up for the lavatory. Once one wanted to go, they all wanted to go. Soon, thought Alice, the girls would begin: they would all be smitten at the same time by the idea rather than by the necessity.

'Now,' Ronnie was shouting, his voice so hoarse with continuous exertion that it cracked on every third or fourth word, 'there's just been a murder. We worked out who did it, but we never got round to dealing with the corpse, did we?'

'That was me,' piped up Martin.

'Yes, we know, but . . . hey, shut that door!'

There was the slam of the door and the voice was muffled. After a few minutes there was a loud squeal and a burst of laughter, then another squeal.

Alice arranged triangular sandwiches on a plate. She could almost follow the progress of the game by the pitch of the shrieks. 'Here's the corpse's hand,' Ronnie would be saying — and then he would pass a rubber glove stuffed with rags along the line in the darkness. 'Here's some of its hair' — and along would go some of the coarse strands from the old sofa which was rotting away in the garden shed. 'And here are its eyeballs.' Two peeled grapes would pass from flinching hand to flinching hand.

Everything was ready for the party tea. She went to the door. It was time Tom came down. She could hear no sound from him.

She went to the foot of the stairs and looked up. 'Tom — are you nearly ready?'

There was no reply. Perhaps he had had to join the end of the queue for the lavatory, having more self-control than the over-excited little boys.

Alice decided to put an end to games for the time being. She went to the sitting-room door and opened it.

'Ah, Mum, close the door.'

'Time for tea.' She switched on the light.

There was a squeal. Then another. And all at once it was hysteria, no longer a joke. One little girl sat staring at what was in her hand and began to scream and scream.

Alice took a step into the room, not believing.

One boy held a severed human hand from which blood dripped over his knees. The girl who could not stop screaming was holding a human eye, squashed and torn. On her left the pimply boy went pale and let a tuft of hair fall between his fingers to the floor.

Alice said: 'No.' Somehow she kept herself upright. 'No. Simon — where's Simon?'

'I'm here, Mrs Jarman.'

The voice was quite calm. She turned to find him standing at one side of the room. She tried to find words. Still cool and detached, he said: 'They locked me in, Ronnie and that one over there locked me in. But I'm all right now. I was let out, and everything's all right now.'

'Then who . . . ?'

She stared at that hideous hand, chopped bloodily off at the wrist. And she recognised it and also the colour of the hair that lay on the floor.

Simon Potter stood quite still as Alice Jarman ran from the room and up the stairs.

She found her husband lying in front of the bedroom cupboard from which he had released the boy. The garden tools lay beside him, splashed with red — the axe that had first smashed in his head and then chopped off a hand, the secateurs that had snipped off a tuft of his hair, and the trowel that had clumsily gouged out his eyes. Simon, pale but content, was now not the only boy in that room downstairs without a father.

DON'T YOU DARE

She had always prophesied contemptuously that he would die before she did. He wouldn't reach fifty, she said. She would be young and attractive enough to marry again, and next time it would be someone she could respect. A real man, next time.

Once he tried to stem the flow of her derision by asking what she wanted him to do if she should happen to go first. She might be involved in an accident. It was only practical to make plans for the children. Michael showed signs of being able to take pretty good care of himself but Candida, at twelve, was sly and difficult, pruriently addicted to reading dubious American thrillers from the public library, or even more dubious paperbacks which she bought with her pocket money in spite of being forbidden to do so. It was her father who had forbidden this. Her mother laughed and told him not to be so stuffy.

'I used to read them by the dozen when I was her age,' she said. 'Everything I could get my hands on. It did me good.'

'Did it?' he rashly said. It was the excuse for her to launch another of her scathing attacks on him.

Candida read half surreptitiously, half defiantly. She thought strange thoughts. She came out with outrageous remarks and then had long spells of mysterious silence. Her mother alternately doted on her and raged at her. She would goad Candida into a tantrum and then hit her across the side of the head and scream at her; and then, just as Robert was sickening with the savagery of it, the two of them would be crying and wrapping their arms round each other. Laura was a great believer in the richness of impetuous swings from one emotion to another, declaring that children loved you more this way than if you were nasty and cold and rational; that everyone, in fact, loved you more this way.

But if there was a sudden end to it, if she was no longer there to sneer and rage and coo, to run things her way because there was no other conceivable way — what then?

'I'd be the one who'd have to marry again,' he said, trying to keep it casual and light-hearted.

'You think anyone would have you?'

'Wouldn't be surprised.'

'You're trying to tell me you've already got someone lined up?'

She would have loved such an excuse to pile even further abuse on him. He was perversely tempted to give her this opportunity: the insults would at any rate be in a different vein from the usual ones. But the whole thing was absurd. He said: 'Of course not. There's nobody.'

'I didn't really imagine there would be.'

'But if I *were* left with the kids — '

'Don't you dare,' she said. 'Marry again? Don't you dare.'

He ought to have known that such a discussion would get nowhere. None of their arguments ever did. And, after all, it was stupid to talk about dying. You didn't plan for death when you were still only in your late thirties.

'In any case,' Laura summed up, 'it won't happen.' Again she trotted out her happy prediction: 'You'll die before I do.'

Yet she was the first to go. On her fortieth birthday she was dead, and he was left with Michael and Candida.

Don't you dare . . .

But he dared.

He married Janet within the year. The quivering tension which Laura had maintained in the house was followed, after her death, by numbness. Now there came warmth and relaxation, a gradual stretching of the limbs and the mind.

Laura had been tall and fair. No matter what the current fashion, she kept her hair long — a beautiful silky mane of which she was swaggeringly proud. Between her shoulder blades she had a streak of faint golden down. She talked about it to friends and even to strangers, and lost no opportunity to exhibit it. In a swimming costume she would turn her back to the sun and writhe gently so that the light could play on this glimmering fur. She implied that there was something very specially, madly sexy about it.

'Robert' — she would wave her hand at her husband with tolerant despair — 'has hardly any hair anywhere. But *anywhere*, my dears.'

She had married Robert in order to escape from a plump, slack, pathetically ignorant mother whom she despised; but after her mother's death she began to talk of her with growing affection. In no time at all she persuaded herself that they had been an ideal mother and daughter and that she ought to have listened more attentively to her mother's shrewd advice.

'I married too young, of course. Not that I blame Robert for that. But I didn't have the chance of doing any of the things I really ought to have done.'

She ought to have been taken up by an international playboy, ought to have gone round the world, ought to have taken up skiing and surfing. She would have been so good: she could sense just how good she would have been. She could have become a tennis champion if Robert hadn't come along and penned her in physically and emotionally, and given her two children. They had nothing in common; it was tragic that she should have discovered this too late.

Next time it would be a real man.

'Given my time over again,' she would laugh to her friends, not finishing the sentence but promising them and Robert and herself that she would, before it was too late, somehow have her time over again.

Her interests waxed and waned. Some were taken up merely to spite Robert and in due course were dropped. Others became obsessions. Whatever Laura discovered was indeed a discovery: nobody had ever known it as she knew it; nobody could understand it as she immediately, intuitively understood it.

Swimming was her greatest passion. It was because of this that Robert slaved to buy the house on the river. Then there was more expense because Laura wanted to have people dropping in from the other houses and from the island and from the plushy cabin cruisers, and they all needed drinks and lots of drinks; and she wanted new clothes so that they could go over and drop in on the houses and the island

and the cabin cruisers for drinks and lots of drinks.

She nagged him about buying a boat. While he worked, she lounged in a bikini on the lawn which sloped down into the river, or swam across to say hello to her friends who weren't ever his friends, or swam along the river and communed with herself and came back reinvigorated, ready to sneer at him yet again.

The river became her personal property. No matter how many boats came and went, no matter how many other people plunged into the water, it was her river. She had used it, so it was hers. She loved it — loved to succumb to it and then to dominate it. She flouted the current by surrendering herself and allowing herself to be pulled towards the weir, knowing the exact moment when she could beat it and escape.

Some evenings in moonlight or pitch darkness she walked down the lawn and into the water and swam across to the lawn on the far side. The major, who lived alone across there, was always glad to offer her a drink. Between them she and

Robert never referred to him as anything other than the major. At first it had been a joke. Then Laura started to talk less jokingly about him and to indicate that he was nice, a sweetie, rather a pet. A real man.

She went over to the major naked but for those two strips of nylon, and invariably stayed for a long time and came back dripping and laughing.

Sometimes Robert knew, but never dared to raise it as a matter of discipline, that Candida was watching from an upper window. Long after she ought to have been asleep she would watch, wide-eyed and attentive, until her mother came out of the water and shook herself and walked arrogantly up the lawn with her hands playing a gentle little tattoo on her scarcely veiled breasts.

On one occasion Laura was prosecuted under some complex waterways by-law. She paid the fine and laughed and made her friends laugh with her. The friends said that one day she would take too big a risk and be swept over the weir on to the harsh, jutting stakes of the breakwater below; but they said it adoringly and didn't really believe it.

Until she went over.

Dead and gone. It was impossible to believe that her vicious, humiliating voice had at last been drowned in the roar of the weir.

'I suppose all marriages go this way.' Robert could not forget it, resonant and repetitive, chattering so lightly and yet so purposefully to as large an audience as she could muster. 'Men! First they leap on you with a glad cry — and then it sort of softens off to a reluctant groan. I suppose it's the same for everyone.'

But she didn't really suppose any such thing. She was sure that somewhere there was a man who could satisfy her. Her hatred was reserved for Robert only, directed tirelessly against Robert.

She was dead. Her hatred must have died with her.

Disconcertingly, it didn't feel like that. She had lived on her resentments and it was inconceivable that their power should have ebbed so swiftly. Her vindictiveness had become a living, physical force stronger than herself. Robert had braced himself against it, his head bowed against it, like a man learning to live with a remorseless prevailing wind. He was not ready to adjust to the fact that the wind had dropped.

If he had died before she did, would she have found it possible to fulfil all those threats she had made to him, all the promises she had made to herself? Without the goad of his presence would she have found any of it worthwhile?

Robert found it easier now to be sympathetic towards her. He could afford to be detached and tolerant. It was easier to assess, to find psychological phrases, to nod understandingly over her disappointments and her knotted agonies. She had made his life hell; but even without him there to storm against, could she ever have been happy?

She was gone. He kept telling himself that she was gone.

Janet was small and dark and softly spoken. She could not have been more different from Laura. Robert had not consciously chosen her because of this, but he wryly admitted to himself that it would not have worked out so rightly and inevitably if she had not been such a complete contrast. He could not help making comparisons; but he did not pass these on to Janet.

She was more interested in her home than Laura had ever been. She found reasons for liking things rather than for disliking them. Ashtrays were emptied, the place was cleaned, towels were not thrown in a heap on the bathroom floor, lights weren't left on and doors weren't left banging. She was tidy without being fussy. The place had a new smell about it, a new glow, a new comfort.

Janet was thirty-five and had not been married before because of a chain of circumstances, not one of which was significant in itself but which, one after the other, had somehow prevented her from settling down. Her parents had gone through various emotional upsets and had both relied on her. Then her father had had a long illness. A job in Wales had been interrupted by the need to look after her brother when he was badly injured in an accident. She spent an unsatisfactory year in Canada. For three years she was involved with a married man and then quietly, resolutely walked out on the situation. If she had been hurt she did not scratch the scars.

After so many years of independence she might well have been diffident and awkward in marriage. Instead, she was graceful and appreciative. Pleasure came to them without having to be desperately pursued.

Laura's body had been magnificent. At forty she had been as sleek and glossy and splendid as a girl of eighteen. In spite of her repeated lamentations she had not suffered from the bearing of two children. Yet for all that flawless beauty she had been cold and brittle and somehow unrewarding.

Janet was . . . oh, he had to say it: Janet was cuddly. Ludicrous word. He thought how Laura would have shrieked with laughter. *Cuddly!* But why not? What was so wrong with that? He didn't have to worry ever again about what Laura would say, because Laura could say nothing.

Still it was hard not to listen, not to wait for that harsh laugh. The echoes were taking a long time to die.

One evening he was late leaving the office and was stuck for twenty minutes in a traffic jam. He began to frame excuses. He would be as reasonable as possible until the row started; then he would have to have a few phrases ready, a few parries.

'Nobody's asking you to apologise' — he could hear Laura saying it — 'for not wanting to come home to me. If you want to stop for a drink, at least have the guts to say so.'

'I didn't stop for a drink. I had a call from Paris.'

'As if it matters. Though you *might* have remembered that Harry and Josie were coming in for a chat. I had to let them go, of course.'

'They could have waited.'

'Until you condescended to arrive? A phone call wouldn't have hurt. A little courtesy — '

'I rang before I left but you must have been out.'

'Liar.'

'I tell you — '

'I don't want you to tell me anything. It's really not worth the fuss. I don't know why you have to make such a pathetic fuss. Do grow up, Robert, dear.'

He rehearsed it; lived through it before it was even begun. And then, as he swung the car down the slope and saw the river curling below him, he realised that he didn't have to practise the scene, didn't have to anticipate every snarled word and impatient twitch of the shoulders: Laura wasn't there; it was Janet now, and Janet wouldn't want to start a petty argument.

He had thought Janet might be intimidated by the children, but she was perfectly at ease. She treated Michael as an equal and was wary yet decisive with Candida.

Michael was in his first year at Sussex University. He had acquired some odd mannerisms, but Janet took them as they came and did not make exaggerated faces as Laura would have done, or grow sweetly patronising as Laura would have done. Michael let it be known that he would eventually become something in television. It was a phrase much used by his friends. He was not sure, any more than they were, of quite what that something was to be; but he wore a pink shirt and a sandy beard in readiness for the day when he was discovered. He spent a holiday in Greece and found an island which could be fully appreciated only by himself and two chosen friends. His favourite word during the first few weeks of this Easter vacation, when he and Janet got to know each other, was 'plasticity'. Last year it had been 'conceptual'. Robert felt that he was a nice healthy boy at heart.

Candida, at the local school, was a heavier responsibility. She lived at home and sulked, brooded, sniggered and grew ecstatic or despairing as she had always done, though with added emphasis, as though to challenge Janet and learn how far she dared go.

Janet coped. She was not domineering and she was not prissy. She did not spy, but she contrived to keep the wrong sort of book out of Candida's hands. She didn't force the pace: she was steady, humorous, and unfaltering.

'I don't believe it,' said Robert one Sunday.

'Don't believe what?'

'The . . . well . . . ' Again he was thinking something naïve — and enjoying it. 'The happiness,' he said. 'That's all — just happiness, just like that.'

She blushed and gave a little pout, shyly repudiating the idea yet loving it. She said: 'You're so sweet.'

Every word they said to each other was true and uncomplicated.

Don't you dare . . .

He had dared and he was happy.

'You're looking well,' his business acquaintances said.

The weeks of summer rolled past and at last he began to accept — really to accept — that Laura was dead. He didn't have to keep saying it to himself any more: it was all right and it didn't need repeating.

For some time he had kept neighbours at arm's length. Then Janet got to know one or two of them. Characteristically, he thought, she picked on the nicer ones and somehow just didn't get round to meeting the rowdier ones.

One Saturday afternoon the major came over for a drink. 'You're looking pretty fit, old boy' he observed. He did not gloat over Janet as he had shamelessly gloated over Laura. He spoke to her with genuine warmth and respect, and for the first time began to treat Robert also with respect.

Lulled into ease and near-complacency, Robert was taken off guard when Laura once again smiled her old, evil smile at him.

He should have been ready. He should have known that the contentment wouldn't last.

Laura was back. Laura was smiling.

It was a hot afternoon. In slacks and a white shirt, Janet sat in the shade of the cherry tree, reading desultorily. Michael sprawled on the grass a few feet away. Every now and then he murmured something to himself or to Janet — from where Robert was working at the water's edge, clearing away some flotsam which had piled up against the bank, it was difficult to tell which. A small aeroplane buzzed drowsily overhead. The weir roared a faint, un-disturbing roar.

Suddenly Michael and Janet began to laugh. Michael pushed himself up on to his knees and leaned towards Janet. He said something quickly, and they laughed again. Their heads turned momentarily towards Robert and then turned away again.

He straightened up and sauntered along the lawn, up the slope to the shade of the tree.

'What are you two plotting?' he asked affectionately.

And there was Laura, gleaming her malice at him. Just one swift, savage gleam of a smile. It took his breath away. He stopped where he was, swaying. He closed his eyes and opened them again. Laura's face had disappeared. It could never have been there; couldn't possibly have been there.

Michael had Laura's eyes. Just for a moment, just in a trick of the light and the dappled shade, Michael's eyes and mouth must have fooled him.

But it hadn't been like that. He knew it hadn't. The brief glimpse had not been of Michael's face. Laura had looked at him and jeered at him not out of her son but out of Janet.

'What's the matter, Robert?' Janet's voice was soft and concerned. She began to get up from her chair. As she emerged into the full blaze of the sun she was his dark, sweet Janet.

An illusion. Nothing more than that. It wouldn't happen again.

Two days later he walked past the open door of Candida's bedroom and saw her sprawled on the bed, reading. He went casually in. 'Not swotting for next term already?'

She drew the edge of the coverlet slowly over the book. The gesture was languid and almost indifferent. She couldn't really be bothered to hide it from him.

'Candida,' he said reproachfully.

She rolled to one side so that he could pull the coverlet back and see the gaudy cover of the book. It was a paperback showing the photographed back view of a girl wearing only a bra. A man bent over her with a whip in his hand, and there was a streak of blood across her right shoulder. It was crude, yet not as crude as paperbacks had once been: it was too glossy and looked photographically, colourfully real.

'What's wrong?' Janet had come along the passage and was standing in the open doorway. Robert prodded the book. 'I thought we'd got over this kind of thing. Honestly, Candida, it's stupid — can't you tell that when you read it?'

'I wouldn't know how stupid it was till I'd had a chance to read it, would I?' she said pertly.

Robert picked it up.

Janet said: 'Do we have to make a big scene about it?'

He froze. There was a crackle in her voice which he recognised. And he saw that this time it wasn't just his imagination. Candida recognised it, too. Candida stared past him, incredulous, and then began to smile, almost hugging herself with glee.

Very carefully he said: 'I thought we'd

agreed there would be no more of this nonsense. Janet — '

'It's nonsense,' she agreed crisply, 'and what harm can it possibly do her?'

'I suppose you used to read them by the dozen when you were her age?'

'Why do you say that?'

'Oh . . . never mind. Never mind.'

Janet shrugged. 'Let her get it out of her system.'

Candida went on staring at her and now held out her hand. Janet took the book from Robert and tossed it back on the bed.

He wanted to talk to Janet. It was imperative that he should talk to her. This whole thing had to be settled today, before trouble overtook them. Yet he found he could not speak. He watched her walk off ahead of him and he couldn't make a move. He wanted to go after her and put his arm round her shoulders and start talking reasonably, as they had always talked until now. But he was afraid. In his fingertips he could already feel how she would shrug him off.

By evening he began to feel safe again.

They sat by the open window in companionable silence. The haze from the river made a silvery dusk, softening the outlines of trees and houses on the far bank. Candida was with friends whose parents would drive her home about half an hour from now. Michael was out on one of his meditative rambles. There was peace.

Robert said: 'Darling . . . '

'Mm?'

'About Candida.'

'Yes. That business earlier today.' Janet put her head on one side as though to catch a puzzling echo. 'You know, I don't quite . . . '

There was the slam of the front door. Michael came in. He flapped a hand amiably at his father and went towards an armchair in the shadows at the end of the room.

Janet said: 'Don't I get a kiss?'

Michael slowly approached the window. Robert tried not to look. He fixed his gaze resolutely on his hands, clasped on his knees. But such resolution could not be sustained. He looked up, looked across at

Janet's profile as she turned towards Michael. The silvery twilight blurred even her dark hair. For one dazzling fraction of a second he saw her face and hands and hair bleached fairer and whiter than death.

Michael bent and kissed her.

'Mm,' said Janet throatily. 'It is nice to have a man about the house.'

Robert got up and reached for the nearest switch. Light flooded from the squat, wide-shaded lamp by the hearth.

'Since you're up,' said Janet, 'you could pour me a drink. Pour us all a drink.'

Robert's hand shook as he got out the glasses. He poured slowly so that there would be time for everything to become normal again. And on the face of it, when they drank, things were normal enough. Janet asked Michael where he had been and Michael muttered in his usual vague way. But there was a strange sense of communication between them: odd references and unfinished sentences which meant nothing to Robert somehow made sense to Janet; a brief little conspiratorial smile flickered to and fro.

Candida was late getting home. The man who brought her apologised, explaining that there had been difficulty getting the car started and that he had stupidly taken a wrong turning and gone miles out of his way. He accepted a drink and left.

Janet swung round upon Candida with her hand raised.

'I told you what time to be back. I told you to make them bring you back in good time.'

'But it wasn't my fault. He's just told you — '

'He's covering up for you. I know your little game. You spin things out as long as you can, and then blame other people.' She struck Candida full across the face. Before Robert could protest, Candida ran from the room. Janet went after her as though to strike her again.

'Janet — stop!'

Robert followed. Janet caught up with the girl at the foot of the stairs and seized her arm. Each of them had a foot on the lowest step. Candida suddenly sagged against Janet. They put their arms round each other and laughed and sobbed weakly.

Above Candida's head, Janet said: 'Let's not have one of your nasty, cold, rational lectures, Robert. You just don't understand girls at all. Girls of any age.'

That night he tried to make love to her. He simply had to restore things to what they had so recently been. But her body had an unyielding softness — a contradiction in terms, an impossibility that was nevertheless a humiliating reality. In the darkness she chuckled. When he fell despairingly away from her she said mockingly: 'Never mind, Robert, dear. Never mind.'

He was glad of the hours he could spend in his office. With staff away on summer holidays, there was a pile-up of work. He welcomed it. It kept him late and he was not sorry to be late. It was not until he was driving home that he began to face up to what lay in wait for him.

Arguments shaped up in his head. He had to work for their living, didn't he? If he stayed late and got home late it was because there was a lot to be done and someone had to do it and he was that someone.

No. No need for arguments. Of course not. Janet was there. Janet would be Janet and nobody else. She would meet him at the door and she would be Janet again.

The arguments seethed over one another, tumbling and twisting.

She would be waiting for him. He kept telling himself that. The old Janet. The only Janet.

When he went into the house there was silence. It was a hot evening, and down here in the river valley it was even more difficult to breathe than it had been in the city.

'Janet?' he called.

There was no reply.

The windows were open on to the garden. Robert went out onto the lawn.

The major was stretched out in a deck-chair on the other side of the river. He waved. And Laura came swimming back across the river as she had so often done. Robert watched, terrified. How could he stop her coming up out of the water, onto the lawn, savage and vengeful?

But it wasn't Laura. It was Janet. She swam noisily and badly. She was floundering as she reached the bank, having to fight the last few yards of the way against the treacherous snatching of the current.

Robert ran to meet her. 'What are you up to? Don't you know how close we are to the weir?'

She stood up, trim and self-possessed in her one-piece black costume. She was breathing hard but she managed to say: 'Pity to have the river here and not use it'

'But you oughtn't to risk it. You're not a good swimmer — are you?'

'I will be.'

'But — '

'Nobody's asking you to come in with me,' Janet snapped. She looked him up and down, then put her hands behind her head and swung languidly round in the evening sunshine. The major waved as she spun to face him. When she had made the full circuit she appraised Robert again. 'The water too cold for you?' she said, and walked past him and into the house.

The house was haunted. The house . . . or perhaps the family. Now he knew it. Haunted not by a separate ghost, an entity, a wandering phantom apart from them, but by a creature indistinguishable from Janet, from Candida, from Michael. They were possessed. This was no mournful shadow waiting in dark corners: it was with them and in them in broad daylight, growing stronger as it fed on them.

Janet took fiercely and repeatedly to the river. One night when Michael and Candida had gone to bed and Robert was yawning, about to comment that it was gone eleven o'clock, Janet abruptly said that she wanted to go out. Just for a little while, to clear her head. Before he could question her, she went up to their room. When she came down she was wearing a wispy bikini. It did not suit her as it had suited Laura: she was an inch or two wrong, slightly too plump, not quite tall enough. But she walked as Laura walked. When she went out down the garden to the darkness of the water, she was Laura.

Robert hurried after her down the lawn.

'You can't. It's mad. At this time of night . . . '

'You can stand by with a lifebelt if it worries you.'

Janet plunged in.

He stood there, helpless. Across the river, lights burned in the windows of the major's house and made a glowing, rippling pool below the bank. Janet swam strongly though clumsily towards it.

Robert turned and looked back at his own house. Michael's bedroom was at one end, Candida's at the other. Their curtains were drawn back. In each window there was a pale, watching face.

Janet was away for over an hour. When she came back she was breathing hard but laughing at the same time. She cupped her hands over her breasts and her fingers beat out a joyful little tattoo on her wet flesh.

She said: 'I've invited the major over to our party next Wednesday.'

'I didn't know we were having a party next Wednesday.'

'Well, we are. I've just decided.'

Among the people she invited were several Robert had not seen for some months. He hadn't known that Janet had even met them. There were the two alcoholics from the island who had always squealed ecstatically over Laura's jokes and then quarrelled at the end of every evening and had to be taken home. There was the old harpy from one of the boats, and a limp young man whom Michael had once claimed to despise but whom he now greeted as a long-lost friend. And there was the couple who lived in sin on the seediest of the nearby boats and made a point of letting everyone know that they were living in sin as though to proclaim their superiority over duller mortals.

Janet had been to have her hair done for the occasion. She had had it dyed blonde. The black softness of it had been converted to a harsh golden helmet.

Robert stared. She did not bother to ask him what he thought about it.

When the major arrived, he, too, stared.

'Like it?' said Janet.

He studied the hair again, then looked her up and down and smacked his lips with exaggerated relish.

'Robert,' said Janet in a tone of patient suffering, 'do keep an eye on the drinks, won't you? Do pretend to be a perfect host.'

It was a long time since he had heard this range and volume of voices. It was the first time for months that glass was trodden into the carpet once more. And the major was touching Janet's arm and gloating, and the couple from the boat were pawing each other and making sure that everyone saw it.

'It's lovely,' said Janet suddenly. She swayed above them with her glass slopping gin over the side. 'I mean, don't you think it's so pretty to watch?' She waved her free arm towards Robert. 'You know, Robert, perhaps we ought never to have got married. Don't you think marriage spoils things?' Now she addressed the assembly, raising her voice and talking them all down. 'You don't get the same kick when it's all been legalised, do you? At least, men don't seem to. Bags of enthusiasm at first, and then all they want is food and someone to sweep the place up. In no time at all they've given up leaping on you with a glad cry and — '

'No,' said Robert. 'Don't say it.'

Janet's eyes widened. They looked at him as they had looked at him year after year, year after terrible year. 'Goodness me, we're on edge this evening, aren't we?'

He tried to get close to her and make a last appeal. But she brushed past him and stood above the major. His arm lay along the arm of his chair. The hair on his wrist was tangled under his watch strap. Janet meditatively stroked the hair up and then smoothed it down again. She looked at Robert. 'Funny, isn't it? Now, Robert hasn't — '

'Stop it.'

'Stop what, Robert, dear?'

The way in which the word 'dear' was wrenched out of her mouth was all too familiar. Her eyes were pools of poison. 'Given my time over again . . . ' Laura had said it but never completed the sentence. She had been given her time over again, and she was just the same; she could do no better than before.

She must not be allowed to do worse.

He said: 'Remember what happened last time.'

Janet said: 'Don't you dare.'

In front of them all he went through it again. They didn't know what he was going to do, so they made no move to stop him; Laura knew, but she wasn't fast enough.

He grabbed the heavy marble ashtray, scattering ash as he swung it. The gilded head ducked and someone screamed — Laura or Janet, he couldn't tell which. Then he slammed the stone edge into the side of that head. The force almost carried him over, but he staggered, gripped the edge of the ashtray, and brought it down again as the head sagged and the body crumpled at his feet. Twice and then three times he was able to lift it and smack it down. Then they were dragging him back.

They didn't let him finish. They couldn't act in time to stop him killing her, but they could stop him carrying her down the darkened lawn and tipping her quietly into the river. This time she would not be carried away down her beloved river. This time she wouldn't suffer the disgrace of being defeated at last by the current and carried over the weir.

Janet did not finish up as Laura had finished up — her beautiful hair tangled, her beautiful body battered and wrenched and beautifully, bloodily pulped against the stakes of the breakwater.

THE END

Other titles in the
Linford Mystery Library:

ZONE ZERO

John Robb

Western powers plan to explode a hydrogen bomb in a remote area of Southern Algeria — code named Zone Zero. The zone has to be evacuated. Fort Ney is the smallest Foreign Legion outpost in the zone, commanded by a young lieutenant. Here, too, is the English legionnaire, tortured by previous cowardice, as well as a little Greek who has within him the spark of greatness. It has always been a peaceful place — until the twelve travellers arrive. Now the outwitted garrison faces the uttermost limit of horror . . .

THE WEIRD SHADOW OVER MORECAMBE

Edmund Glasby

Professor Mandrake Smith would be unrecognisable to his former colleagues now: the shambling, drink-addled erstwhile Professor of Anthropology at Oxford is now barely surviving in Morecambe. He has many things to forget, although some don't want to forget him. Plagued by nightmares from his past, both in Oxford and Papua New Guinea, he finds himself drafted by the enigmatic Mr. Thorn, whom he grudgingly assists in trying to stop the downward spiral into darkness and insanity that awaits Morecambe — and the entire world . . .

DEATH BY GASLIGHT

Michael Kurland

London has been shocked by a series of violent murders. The victims are all aristocrats, found inside locked rooms, killed in an identical manner. Suspecting an international plot, the government calls in the services of Sherlock Holmes. Public uproar causes the police to set visible patrols on every street; fear of the murderer looks like putting the criminal class of London out of business! They in turn call in the services of Holmes's nemesis, Professor James Moriarty. What will happen when the two titans clash with the killer?